Death of An Aristocrat

A Lucy Anne Trotter Mystery

By

Anya Wylde

Acknowledgment

For John who has spent countless hours reading and editing my books. He has wielded the red pen with abandonment, yet, boosted my writer's ego whenever it floundered. Without him, I would be lost.

For Marcus and Daniel who bring laughter and fun into my life. These little ones have taught me more than I could have imagined.

For Portia, my ball of fluff, whose reassuring weight I constantly feel on my feet as I write.

Thank you, Fiona, Jane Daugherty, Angie Joy, Simone, Lori George, Betsy Loran, Jennifer, Casey Jones, Sharon Leach, Candi Foster, Celeste Meehan, Susan York, Barbara, and Helena for your all your help. I truly appreciate it.

Contents

Prologue

The dark stone walls and the fat toad-like structure of Gopshall contrasted sharply with the stunning white country landscape.

Its wart-like protrusions were dusted with snow, while the windows glinted icily at the wild, picturesque woodland surrounding it.

It was snowing again, and what began as soft, delicate flakes dancing in the sunlight, swiftly turned vicious as it continued to fall, fast and heavy.

The clouds darkened, and the thick snowy carpet began to rise higher and higher.

The wind picked up speed and whipped through the grounds turning snow and dirt into a chaotic whirlwind. It proceeded to sweep through the country, testing the foundations of English homes by slamming into walls and windows with its frosty tail.

The sun fought a brave battle with the clouds but failed miserably. It turned into a pale version of itself and plunged the country into darkness.

After three days of turbulence, the wind, at last, ran out of breath and the clouds dissipated.

England slumped in relief, its terrain frozen, treacherous and deathly quiet.

After a hushed night, people poked their icy noses out of doors and windows and tutted at the mounds of dirty snow dotting the land.

People in the country found twigs, leaves and mud swirled

through the heaps of snow, while the Londoners were greeted with the sight of fish bones, corpses of mice and colourful hats poking out of little grey snowy hills.

The spectacle on the ground may have been vastly different between the town and countryside, but the clear morning sky looking down on all of England sported the same pink and gold victorious smirk.

The end of the storm was a matter of joy to most people.

The privileged inhabitants of Gopshall, on the other hand, were sorry the storm was over so soon. For them, it had been an amusing diversion, and they wished, most fervently, that another one was brewing somewhere, ready to strike them as soon as possible.

∞∞∞

"Lady Willoughby?" The valet cowered near the door.

"Is my husband up yet?"

"I am not sure—" He swallowed.

Lady Catherine Willoughby's delicate head whipped up like an Indian cobra ready to strike. Her golden ringlets danced in the firelight, and her baby blue eyes frosted over. Her sharp nose seemed to get pointier as she narrowed her gaze.

The valet's eyes darted from the vase lying dangerously close to Lady Willoughby's lovely fingertips to her extraordinarily broad forehead. He swayed.

"I am sorry." The valet took a nervous step back. His skin was deathly pale, and he spoke as if in a trance, "but I need to discuss an urgent matter with his lordship. I was hoping to find him here .... Perhaps he is still in bed—"

"What is it, George?" Lord Willoughby shuffled past the valet almost knocking him over. He looked like a spotty egg which had cracked at the bottom to allow a pair of spindly legs to slip through. His eyes were shot through with tiny red veins, and his colour was a trifle orange green.

He went and stood by the fireplace and sighed as the heat warmed him up. He leaned against the pink velvet armchair and carefully moved his eyeballs from his wife's face to the valet's, expertly avoiding looking at the cakes and slices of bread lying on the table.

Lady Willoughby kept her eyes glued to the flickering flames. She stared so intently that it seemed as if she was willing the fire to burn a touch more enthusiastically, just enough to leap out and sting her husband's giant bottom.

"Can we please speak privately?" the valet begged.

"You can speak in front of her," Lord Willoughby said, who was in no mood to navigate his way to the study while feeling like a pirate who had lost his sea legs. He had drunk only a thimble of the brandy last night, and, yet, he felt like he had soaked his entire body in a gin-filled tub—"

"It's a delicate matter."

Lord Willoughby leaned harder on the chair. He waved his hand, "Go on. No one is delicate here."

Lady Willoughby placed a pale hand on her chest and gasped.

"No need to be dramatic, my dear. George knows all about your nerves. Thick as iron rods." He chuckled. "Sympathise with *my* nerves instead. They are feeling a touch shattery this morning. They seem to be swimming about like confused, drunken worms—"

"Lord Beazley is dead," the valet blurted out.

Stunned silence greeted his announcement.

When no one spoke the valet repeated himself,

"Oh," Lord Willoughby's legs gave out, and he sank into the armchair. "You must be mistaken. Either that or I am still asleep."

"I found him in the woods. Shot through the heart . . . blood all over the snow. I-I dragged his body here."

"Here," Lady Willoughby screeched. It seemed her husband was right about her sensibilities. It had taken her but a moment to recover her wits. "What do you mean you dragged the body here? We just laid new carpets—"

"He is lying on the doorstep," the valet clarified.

"How can you worry about the carpet, Catherine, when our guest is dead?" Lord Claybrook, the handsome younger brother of Lord Willoughby, demanded from the doorway.

His height and muscular frame instantly dwarfed the puce and pink morning room. His dark, intelligent eyes darted from his brother to his wife, and his face tightened as it fell on the latter.

Lord Willoughby sank deeper into the chair and drew up his knees. His eyelashes flickered nervously as he stared up at his brother.

On the other hand, a swift change came over Lady Willoughby. Her bones softened and turned fluid in the pink morning dress. She appeared fragile, seductive and helpless. No one would believe, looking at her trim waist, that she had birthed three children.

"Oh, you wouldn't understand," Lady Willoughby said, as she twisted in her seat to present him with her favoured profile. "It's so difficult to clean. Tell them, Rosie."

Her maid did not respond as she had swooned at the news of the murder and landed on the lemon cake.

Lord Claybrook ignored Lady Willoughby, pulled out a flask from his robe and looked around for a cup. Finding none, he tipped some brandy into an oriental blue vase and thrust it into the valet's hand. "Drink up. You are trembling."

"You are not mistaken?" Lord Willoughby asked again.

The valet swallowed the drink and shook his head.

"Bring him into the parlour. Bring the body, I mean," Lord Willoughby squeaked. "This is a nasty business. Father will not be pleased."

"Bring him in?" Lady Willoughby thundered. "Certainly not. It's not like he is family."

"But Catherine—" Lord Willoughby pleaded.

"William, a dead body in Gopshall Manor? I will never be able to sleep again."

"How can you be so cruel and selfish?" Lord Claybrook

snapped. "A man is dead, and you are asking us to leave him on the doorstep—"

"It's not like he can feel the cold," Lady Willoughby snapped back. "He is dead. Be sensible."

"Bring the body in," Lord Claybrook said, looking Lady Willoughby dead in the eye. "A man has been murdered, and only someone heartless could have done it."

"You think I killed him?" she asked, springing to her feet in outrage.

"The snow is thick, making this place inaccessible. Which means that someone in this house killed Lord Beazley."

"Are you saying we have a murderer in our midst, Richard?" Lord Willoughby asked in horror.

"That is exactly what I am saying, William."

The second housemaid, holding a silver tray laden with coffee, cream and strawberry jam, collapsed on the newly laid carpets with a poignant thud.

Chapter One

Lucy Anne Trotter hung upside down from a tree. The rope bit into her ankles while the arrow, which had narrowly missed her right ear lobe, quivered on a thick branch next to her.

Her skirt and petticoats had fallen over her eyes, so she carefully uncovered her head and stuck what she could of the grey woollen skirt between her knees.

Her ankles and calves were still on display and probably her entire bottom as well, but propriety be damned. In this weather, her chances of freezing to death were far more imminent than offending delicate sensibilities.

Besides, as far as she knew, Lord Adair kept only a handful of servants. She recalled meeting his valet . . . or had he been a butler? He was an odd sort with his brown hair tied on top of his head with a bit of red ribbon and fanned out like a bird's tail.

She frowned, shook her head and tried to focus on more urgent matters like saving her skin.

She felt remarkably calm considering she had just walked into a trap, but then she had spent all her life jumping from one pickle to the next with nary a rest in between.

Why, when she had lived in the orphanage, she had survived many predicaments, diseases and hardships. She was small and hadn't needed much food, which helped, as did her tenacity to survive. Besides, she was like a demented bee; busy and happy.

She disliked being miserable, which confounded most people. Humans, she had realised at an early age, would rather wallow in self-pity and swim in a river of misery than put on a smile and enjoy all that life had to offer.

She chuckled as she recalled sending love letters from the miserly cook to the strictest and meanest teacher in the school after being unfairly punished. The result had been unexpected. The cook and teacher fell in love and, love, as it has a way of doing, softened their hard edges and, henceforth, they became far more pleasant to deal with.

She sighed. Oh, to be in love, get married and have a bunch of children.

Her legs went numb, yanking her back to the present. She really should be getting on and saving her neck.

She took a deep breath and let out a blood-curdling scream. "Heeeelppp!"

Her horse, tied to a majestic oak tree, neighed sympathetically. No one else responded.

She searched the grounds of the Lockwood mansion for any sign of life. The mansion's rooftops were covered with snow, like thick icing on a dense, sweet fruit cake. The grass below shimmered like candied sugar in the bright winter sun, and dark, leafless trees stood tall and straight like caramel sticks, proud to be a part of the Lockwood family land.

Her stomach growled. She was hungry.

A small stream winked at her from behind a snow-dusted hedgerow. Next to the stream was a thin path strewn with dry twigs that meandered away into the distance. She spotted a thawing pond, green with a crust of grey ice, a stable covered in frosted ivy, and a cream gazebo with lovely arched windows, but nothing farther, since her eyesight was poor.

The air was still and heady with the scent of witch hazel and winter jasmine, but so cold that it was difficult to breathe it in. The sharp air burned her nostrils, and she took shallow breaths, desperately wishing for the sun to shine a tad bit brighter.

She wrenched her gaze from the wild, hypnotic landscape and willed the thick wooden doorway of the mansion to fly open.

Nothing happened.

She hollered again, but a sudden gust of icy breeze stole most of her words away.

She was hungry, cold and getting desperate. The snow had soaked her clothes, gloves and thin boots and was now working on her second layer of woollen socks. Her exposed behind felt like a block of ice.

She began to panic. Perhaps this time she wouldn't be able to save herself. Perhaps, this was it … her last and final pickle.

She had to survive. She couldn't die yet, not now when she had just discovered that her parents may not have died in a fire.

She recalled the anonymous letter she had received a while ago; a few lines that simply asked her to search for the truth about her family.

She needed answers. So many answers. To die without knowing who she was to begin with … would be tragic.

She opened her mouth and with renewed vigour began to scream like a demented banshee.

The nearest window popped open, and a gorgeous voice like liquid honey asked, "Who in the blazes is making that confounding racket?"

"Me," Lucy caught her skirts that had escaped from between her knees and yanked them off her face in relief.

"Me who?"

"Lucy."

"Lucy, who?"

"Lucy Anne Trotter."

Lord William Ellsworth Hartell Adair, the Marquess of Lockwood, international spy, renowned national hero, the saviour of the King and Regent, and the most handsome man in England, paled at the news.

"Good lord, it cannot be."

Chapter Two

Lord Adair took her to a dusty blue and grey parlor. It had an impossibly high ceiling with dramatic scenes painted on it. In splashes of gold, red and Prussian blue, it depicted fantastical creatures from Greek mythology.

The furnishings were sparse and dusty, the carpet thick and dense and the high arched windows were framed with thick blue and silver brocade curtains that matched the chaise longue.

An odd scent permeated the room. After a moment, Lucy realised that it was a mixture of old books, whiskey and leather. A disturbing and unfamiliar masculine scent that made her nose twitch.

She moved her skirts to make room for him, and he sat down next to her.

The fire crackled in the grate, and they warily eyed one another.

He wore a green silk robe that skimmed and flowed over his muscles. His dark eyes, framed by long, thick lashes were sleepy and hooded, while his fine aristocratic features appeared a little roguish in the pale early morning light. His hair was a touch dishevelled, something she instinctively knew would bother him if he became aware of it.

He was handsome . . . far too attractive for the likes of her.

She shivered.

He suddenly sprang up and left the room.

She sat on the very edge of the seat, gripping her skirts in confusion.

Had she offended him somehow? Did she smell funny? She discreetly sniffed herself. She smelled like a snowy soup of spruce, twigs and rabbit droppings.

He returned just as abruptly as he had left, carrying a thick white fur blanket. He threw it over her shoulders, making her squeak.

She gingerly held the edges close to her shivering body, worried that the dirt from her dress would stain the stark white fur, but the warmth it afforded was too inviting for her to refuse it. She wrapped it around herself, as tight as she could, and wished she could lean back and enjoy it properly.

He stoked the fire until it blazed hot and bright and rang for refreshments.

She twisted her blue fingers, feeling wary and uncomfortable. She felt like an unwanted intruder, who by rights should be sent to the kitchens to be seen to by the servants and not treated the way he was treating her . . . like a lady worthy of his personal attention.

She glanced up to see him searching her face. Could he read her mind? A lot of people thought he had all sorts of strange powers. They said he could predict the future, read minds, fight a hundred men at once. Surely, it wasn't true?

She looked away from his dark knowing gaze. He was *far* more handsome than anyone had the right to be and *had* accomplished things no regular man could.

He sighed, and she opened her mouth to ask him a question when she realised her teeth were chattering. She clenched her jaw and dropped her lashes.

"You will feel better soon," he said gently.

She sneezed and nodded; the kindness in his voice made her eyes prickle.

He took out a clay pot from his pocket and opened it. She slid her eyeballs towards it and eyed it curiously. It contained a yellow paste with an earthy scent.

"Hold still," he said and began applying the salve on the slight nick on the tip of her ear. The arrow had, in fact, managed to graze it. The cold had numbed the pain, and she hadn't realised it until she began to thaw.

She stared resolutely at his chin, still as a mouse, barely breathing. He didn't need to tell her to hold still, she thought nervously. Being this close to him was bound to make any woman in England freeze in delight.

Except what she was feeling was not pleasant. It was a mixture of fear, apprehension and awe.

He was Lord William Ellsworth Hartell Adair, the marquess of Lockwood, while she was an orphan with questionable roots. He could tie her up and toss her into the dungeon or shoot her dead and say he had done it for England, and no one would doubt his word.

She shivered. She had sought his help once, but at the time she had been newly released into the world by the reluctant head-mistress of the orphanage, The Brooding Cranesbill.

She had been naïve and heartbreakingly silly.

But within the last few months, she had learned a few lessons. She had learned that the world was far more hostile than she had thought, it was impossible to control the events or people around her and most importantly, the likes of her needed to stay away from aristocrats.

And yet, here she was, sitting in front of a blue blood, who was not only a breath away from her, but also touching her earlobe.

An exceedingly lucky earlobe.

She could imagine how jealous the ladies of the *ton* would be if they ever discovered that a simple governess had her cold ear-lobe tended to by none other than Lord Adair.

He cleared his throat. "Did you want to ask me something?"

"Eh?"

"Stop staring."

She blinked furiously. "I wasn't staring. I was thinking. And while I was thinking, my eyes just happened to land on you. I didn't register your features. It was all a vague blur. Rather my mind was elsewhere—"

"Miss Trotter."

"Hmm?"

"You are blithering like a fool. Have some tea."

She glared at him. "I do not blither, and I see no teapot."

He threw his eyes up at the ceiling as if appealing to the centaurs painted on it to save him from a dimwit.

"Did you want to ask me something?" he repeated slowly.

"Did you see my unmentionables?" she blurted out and then clapped her hands to her mouth.

"What?"

She was asking herself the same question. What in the world had made her say that? Had her head frozen, thawed and then turned to mush? Or had the damage been caused by dangling upside down for an extended period?

He wiped his fingers on the rim of the clay pot, placed it on the table, and then took out a cigar from his pocket. He waited for her response, his eyes twinkling.

She glared at him. He had all day to roll around the sofa, smoking cigars and taking snuff, but she was running out of time. She took a deep breath and said in a rush, "I was dangling upside down, and my skirts were over my head. Did you look?"

He cut his cigar and said mildly, "My dear, *that* is not a very ladylike question."

"So, you *did* look!" she gasped, turning bright red.

"What are you doing here?" he tossed the cigar and watched it roll off the table and land on the carpet.

The butler entered just then and stepped on it. He glanced down at the squished cigar and the smear of tobacco and ignored it.

Any butler, worth his salt, would be asking for a maid to come running with a mop. She frowned.

Lord Adair didn't seem to mind his incompetence.

The butler—she assumed that's who he was— deposited a tea tray on the table with a crash. A bit of the tea leapt out of the cup and onto the tarnished silver tray.

His hair was tied with a blue ribbon today, she noted, and had been arranged to resemble the tail of an aquatic warbler. She wanted to leap up, throw his ribbon in the fire and scold him for taking advantage of a good man like Lord Adair.

The butler, in turn, eyed her curiously, his bony face full of harsh lines.

Lord Adair added a splash of brandy to the cup and handed it to her. The butler took that as a signal to depart.

Lucy swallowed the sweet, hot tea gratefully. The brandy warmed her and soothed some of her indignation towards the butler, and the tiny, hard wafers that he apologetically offered her, filled her stomach and made her feel much better.

"Are you ready to speak?" Lord Adair asked.

Lucy straightened in her seat and nodded her head. "I am ever so grateful that you found me the governess' job at Gopshall . . . but—"

"But?"

"The children are spawns of the devil. All five of them."

"You wanted to be a governess. You said you liked children."

"I like most children. I have seen some awful ones at the orphanage, but even they would do anything for an apple slice. While Lord Willoughby's children are ungrateful little beasts stuffed up with meat and pudding—"

"It is your job to get them to behave."

"But I was tortured," she said imploringly. "They put toads in my bed, cow dung in my pillowcase, cut up my favourite piece of lace and stole all my puddings!"

"Did you complain to Lady Willoughby?"

"I did, but she said not to bother her with such trifles. So, I did what anyone in my position would do. I put toads in their bed, cow dung in their pillows and stole their puddings."

His eyes widened. "So, they threw you out?"

"Not precisely. Lady Willoughby was angry, but she seemed more upset about my sewing skills than my method of revenge. I cannot sew as you can see from my own dress. One sleeve is longer than the other. Somehow when I come near a sewing basket, my fingers sever from my mind, and the result is usually deplorable. I assure you, that is my *only* fault. I am an excellent baker, I speak French, write exquisite letters—"

He held up his hand.

Lucy hurried on. "Lady Willoughby asked me to alter her dress, and by the time I was done, some crucial bits of the dress went missing . . . like the bodice and a bit of the skirt."

"And they threw you out?

"Not precisely. Right after Lady Willoughby assaulted my ears, one of the devils . . . I mean, children, refused to go to bed. He is the eldest of the lot and hadn't forgiven me for the toads and the dung, so I was chasing him around the house—"

Lord Adair pressed his lips together and gestured for her to continue.

She nodded and continued bravely, "And then he ran into the study. His father, Lord Willoughby, was already in the room, lurking by the bookshelf, gnawing on a chicken leg and drunk as a wheelbarrow. Lady Willoughby doesn't like him to overeat, so he hides in the library and eats a second dinner. He is small and round and looks like he would burst any moment, so I suppose she is right in a way ...."

"Get on with your tale."

"The young lad ran past his father, knocking the chicken leg off his hand and hid behind the bookshelf. I naturally ran after the boy. I had to. He could have got his grubby hands all over the books."

"And?"

"Well, the floor is marble. Did you know the servants polish it every day so that it gleams? I try and see my reflection in it sometimes, but somehow the light is never right. Anyhow, I ran after the brat. Did I mention the chicken?

"The chicken he was eating that was knocked off by his son. Yes, you did," he said, closing his eyes as if he already knew what was coming next.

"You have a good memory. I, however, do not. I forgot about the chicken and next thing you know I step on it, slip and go flying in the air. Lord Willoughby tried to help me by grabbing my shoulder, but my flight was too swift, filled with too much power. I barraged into him and knocked him off his feet, and then I found myself lying on top of him while he ended up underneath me."

"Both of us were gasping very loudly trying to get our breath and our bearings sort of thing, and just then Lady Willoughby and her two maidservants walked in. I heard her tell them to lock me in the room. She was going to take all my money away for I deserved none of it and then decide my punishment."

"So, you ran away?"

"Not precisely. I thought Lord Willoughby would explain the situation to his wife and all would be forgiven—"

"Come to the point, Miss Trotter."

"Lord Beazley was a guest at Gopshall, and he was murdered yesterday morning, and they said . . . I did it."

Chapter Three

Lord Adair poured her another cup of tea. "Did you do it?"

"No! Why would I kill a stranger?"

"And yet, Lord and Lady Willoughby think you are to blame."

"That's because they think the bullet was meant for Lord Willoughby. They think I tried to seduce him because of the whole chicken incident. When that didn't work, they said I flew into a passionate rage and shot him. Also, the fact that someone was murdered at the last house I worked in seemed to convince them that I was guilty."

"Why do they think the bullet was meant for Lord Willoughby?"

"Because Lord Beazley was wearing Lord Willoughby's clothes when he was shot and since the two of them are of a similar build, the murderer could have mistaken one for the other."

She put her hand up, "I know what you are going to ask me next."

When he remained silent, she continued, "Lord Beazley arrived at our house a few days ago. His valet was meant to follow in another carriage, with his belongings. But it began snowing, and the valet was presumably held back by the storm, and Lord Beazley was left with nothing to wear. Lord Willoughby kindly lent him his own clothes. They even wagered who would get the best silk robe the first night they played cards."

Lord Adair crossed his ankles and leaned back. He seemed

lost in thought, and she fell silent.

She watched the flickering flames, feeling uneasy. The burning logs were spluttering and shooting sparks, a few even flew out of the grate and made for her skirts. She took a deep breath to calm her nerves and banish the sudden image of Lockwood going up in flames dancing in her mind's eye.

He finally spoke. "I would have liked to keep you here a little longer and ensure you haven't suffered any ill effects after your adventure this morning, and perhaps, ask the physician to take a look at you . . . feed you something more hearty—"

"I am not a child," she scowled.

He continued as if she hadn't spoken, "But, I think we need to head to Gopshall Manor right away."

He slid off the sofa and began rummaging underneath it. A moment later, he emerged, holding a walking stick. It was black with a silver cheetah head. He grasped the crown and sprang to his feet.

"We must make haste, *child*," he said, with a slight smile. "It will be much harder for me to get to the truth of the matter if we arrive Gopshall Manor after Lord Willoughby informs the duke that you murdered Lord Beazley."

"You will not let them hang me, will you?" Lucy clutched his arm in fear.

He stared down at her for a moment, his face softened. "If you haven't killed him, then I will do my best to prove your innocence."

Lucy's shoulders sagged in relief.

He left her alone after that to plan for their departure. He urged her to sit closer to the fire and dry as much of her clothes as she could.

She didn't dare move closer to the grate, but she did spread her skirts out and took her shoes off to dry her feet. At some point, she fell asleep on the armchair.

A light tap on her shoulder woke her up.

The late morning sun was streaming into the room like fat ribbons of light. She blinked and rubbed her eyes when she spotted Lord Adair peering down at her.

He was wearing a dark blue waistcoat under a heavy grey woollen coat. The gilt buttons at his collars and cuffs glinted in the light. He also wore buckskin breeches, ribbed woollen stockings and riding boots. On his head sat a dark grey hat trimmed in black satin, and he held the cheetah walking stick. A soft pink pashmina lay draped over his arm.

He held the shawl out to her now.

She reached out and absently touched it, thinking it all a wonderful dream when, all at once, she recalled the events of the previous day. She hurriedly sat up and smoothed her hair, feeling embarrassed.

Had she drooled?

Egad! what if she had drooled on Lord Adair's cushions. She frantically patted the corners of her mouth and then began checking the chair for any sign of damage. Had she smeared dirt all over it?

"What on earth are you doing?" He caught her hand to still her.

She froze like a bird caught in a snare. "I," she swallowed. "I . . . nothing."

"Take the shawl and come along. The carriage is ready."

"It's too lovely," she hesitated.

"Your coat is an appalling colour. You look like a starved rat with missing fur in it. Just take the deuced shawl, girl, and hurry up."

She leapt up to do his bidding. She threw the shawl around her shoulders, yanked her shoes back on her feet and raced after him.

The landau, with its gleaming glass windows and soft cream leather seats, beckoned her invitingly. The horses neighed impatiently and stamped their feet, prompting her to quicken her steps.

The butler helped her in, squinting suspiciously at her as he did so.

"Barnaby, ask the captain to stay until I return," Lord Adair addressed the butler, who was also, she realised later, the coach driver.

Barnaby, she smiled. The name didn't suit him, but it did make him seem less threatening. And who was the captain?

Lord Adair sat down opposite her and rapped the walls. After a moment, the carriage lurched forward and began moving.

"My horse," she suddenly gasped.

"—Is harnessed to this carriage," he said calmly. "He will be returned to Gopshall where he belongs."

"I didn't mean to say he was mine. It was a figure of speech."

"I understand."

"The kittens?" she asked after a moment.

"Ah, the ones you left with me before resuming your new position. They are thriving. I gave them to Captain. She is delighted with them."

"Captain?"

"My cook."

"Oh."

A raven swooped in just then and settled on Lucy's shoulder.

"Spinoza! You followed me," she cried in delight.

He shook his head, wryly. "A pet raven. They are solitary creatures, but this one seems sociable. Perhaps, he is just an enormous crow."

"Hush, you will hurt his feelings," she admonished, then immediately bit her lip. She really should remember who sat in front of her and guard her tongue.

He leaned forward. "Lucy?"

Her name on his lips struck through her like a lightning bolt. Her eyes flew to his, and she was taken aback by the intensity in his gaze.

"Don't lose your courage," he said softly. "Don't lose your fire and become one of them. Don't fear me."

It sounded almost like a plea. It confused her. She nodded, even though she didn't entirely understand what he meant.

He didn't speak much after that and remained lost in thought for the rest of the drive.

The journey which should have taken an hour at most, took them three hours since the footman and the carriage driver had to stop frequently to shovel the snowdrifts blocking their path.

The delay was making her nervous. She felt hot, uncomfortable and slightly sick. She couldn't blame the carriage for her queasy stomach since it was well sprung.

"I have never seen it snow so heavily," she finally broke the silence.

"It is unusual."

"Frightening," she sneezed. "That drift is halfway up the tree."

"It's a small tree."

She rummaged in her pocket and pulled out a piece of fruit cake wrapped in a handkerchief and offered it to Lord Adair. "It will warm you up. The raisins are soaked in rum."

He politely declined. "I am fine. Tell me about Lord Beazley. When did he arrive, what mood was he in? How did the household react when they saw him? Everything that you can remember."

She picked at the crumbs thoughtfully, glad he had given her something to do. "Three days ago, late in the evening, I was in the garden trying to drag the children indoors. It was cold, and the light was fading fast when a carriage rolled into the driveway. We paused to watch a portly man pop out and make his way up the stairs. The butler let him in, and that was all I saw of him that day. The cook informed me late that night that the new guest was Lord Beazley. The following two days he spent cloistered in the study with Lord Willoughby. I don't eat with the family, so I didn't spot him at dinner either. The next thing I know, they were accusing me of murdering the man."

"Is that all you can tell me? Did anyone appear different after his arrival? More agitated, happier or anything unusual at all?"

Lucy shook her head. "I don't have much to do with the family. The children are difficult and take up most of my time. As far as I know, nothing changed."

"Tell me about the people in the house."

"As you know, I mind Lord Willoughby's five children. Three

are from his current wife, Lady Catherine Willoughby, and the rest from his previous wife, who died tragically in childbirth. Apart from them, Lord Willoughby's widowed younger brother, Lord Claybrook has come to visit with his two children and their governess, Miss Jane Peyton. Lord Aston, the owner of Gopshall Manor and Lord Claybrook and Lord Willoughby's father, is also a resident, though, rarely spotted. The servants—"

He held up his hand. "Enough, for now. Thank you, Miss Trotter."

He closed his eyes and tilted his head back on the leather seat.

She wasn't sure if he was thinking or snoozing. She watched his handsome profile, indulging her eyes for a moment. She tried to set aside her worries and have faith in him.

It was difficult. She was asking him to go against his own sort and help her. What if he handed her over to Lord Willoughby, the moment they set foot in Gopshall Manor? What if his kindness was a ruse?

She stared out of the window, her stomach roiling with emotion. She had no choice. Going to Lord Adair had been a desperate gamble, and all she could do now was to let the cards play out and hope for the best.

The horses trotted through the snow, making puffs of white dust on the ground. The breeze brushed over the powdered ice creating swirls of white smoke and mist. It was beautiful and eerie at the same time.

She took a large bite of the cake and mimicked Lord Adair's pose. The rest of the answers lay in Gopshall manor, and she hoped he would be able to dig them out and prove her innocence.

Chapter Four

Jane

Miss Jane Peyton unfolded the newspaper and read in a soft, steady voice,
'The fete held to celebrate the prince becoming a regent turned out to be an extraordinary affair.

Rumour has it that thousands arrived to join the party. The Regent does not command such devotion, but we rather think it was curiosity that drove people to appear at the gates. The good people of England may have assumed that the 'regent' was, in fact, a newly purchased curiosity.

We also heard that many men broke their limbs, and some women lost their clothes during the lavish party. How it all came about is still a mystery.

People with delicate sensibilities judiciously avoided the event since they didn't think it was right to celebrate the fact that the king had lost his marbles.

In other news, Lady V.M has eloped with her second footman.'

Lady Willoughby frowned. "I am glad I didn't go. It sounds horrid."

It took a moment for Jane to stop blushing and regain her composure. The gossip columns were shocking. She set aside the newspaper and quickly picked up her embroidery and set to work.

"You are far more accomplished than that awful Miss Trotter," Lady Willoughby eyed Jane's small, dark head fondly. "You keep Claybrook's children wonderfully well behaved. I have never heard *you* complain, and your company is soothing. I wish I could steal you away from Claybrook. I suppose it's your breeding coming through. A lady, no matter how impoverished, will *always* be a lady."

Jane's hand slipped, and the needle pierced her skin. She bit back a cry and sucked her thumb.

"I hope Miss Trotter is caught," said Rosie, the lady's maid. She set the teapot down on the table and tutted. "I never liked the look of her, Miss."

"Are you certain she killed him?" Jane asked carefully.

Lord Willoughby walked in just then. "Who else could it be?" he asked irritably. "She ran the moment we questioned her. If she had been honest, she would have stayed and proved her innocence."

He took a seat opposite his wife and glanced over at Jane. His eyes raked her form quickly and expertly, pausing at her full lips and small waist.

Jane shrank in her seat. She was not beautiful like Lucy but was the sort that grew on you like an exotic delicacy. At first, she appeared plain, and then her smile would light up her brown eyes and make her seem almost pretty. Her skin was clear and her mouth sweet and inviting. Her figure was slim, and her clothes always neat.

Lord Willoughby accepted a cup of tea from Rosie and continued, "I am glad we discovered the culprit so quickly. I don't think you would have been able to handle such nasty business had it gone on any longer, my dear."

Lady Willoughby pushed a plate of sandwiches towards her husband. Her eyes narrowed in disgust as he took two and stuffed them in his mouth.

"You are so delicate, my lady," he said, bits of bread spraying out of his mouth. A piece of chicken attached itself to his uneven beard and stuck fast. "You shouldn't have to deal with such an awful business. I am surprised you didn't take to bed for a fortnight."

Lady Willoughby pinned her eyes on the fire; her hands curled around her skirts and her mouth pressed into a thin line. He was mocking her.

Jane wrapped her shawl tighter around her shoulders and bent even lower over her embroidery. She wished she could dive into the bed of flowers she was sewing and disappear.

As a governess, she was in a peculiar position. Unlike the servants, she didn't have to flit around like a shadow, doing her best to stay invisible. She could speak to the lady of the house and command a little more respect.

Yet, when the men came into the room, she faded into the background and became privy to intimate conversations, ugly fights and dangerous secrets.

This was one of those moments. She could feel the couple readying for battle. The air felt heavy and oppressive as if a giant elephant was floating on top of them, ready to bury them at any moment.

Jane rubbed the back of her neck and glanced at the door. The children were asleep in the nursery. Perhaps, she should check on them.

She was about to get up when the door flew open, and Mr Underhill, the butler, came charging in. "Heyounder," he gasped.

"Eh?" Lord Willoughby blinked at him.

The butler clutched the door handle, his finger's white with pressure.

"He found Lucy," the butler repeated slowly.

"Where?" Lady Willoughby sat up.

"Who found her," Lord Willoughby demanded at the same time.

"She arrived in a carriage not a moment ago," The butler exclaimed.

"Carriage?" she asked frowning.

"It bears the mark of Lockwood."

"The Marquess," Lady Willoughby shot to her feet. "Lord Adair!"

"It cannot be," Lord Willoughby trembled.

"We are not prepared to receive him," Lady Willoughby shrieked. "The house, the guest room . . . My hair! My hair! Stall him. He must not see me like this! Rosie quick, bring me a comb, the pot of 'Blooming Roses', and 'Midnight Soot'. Hurry!"

Jane couldn't help herself from asking, "Does this mean Lucy is innocent?"

Lord and Lady Willoughby spun on their feet like wooden tops and stared at her in horror.

"What's gotten into you, Miss Peyton?" Lord Willoughby snapped. "No doubt, Lord Adair found her and brought her back to face justice."

"Didn't he recommend her?" Jane persisted; her voice trembled just a touch.

"His father was an old friend of my father's," Lord Willoughby said impatiently. "We meet in parliament sometimes and exchange greetings. He heard about my need for a governess and sent her along. He is not her guardian and has no reason to protect her. His loyalty is to our family, not to some lowly governess."

Jane flushed and looked away.

Lady Willoughby smoothed her skirts and ran a tongue around her sharp, yellow teeth. She peered at her reflection on the back of a spoon and said irritably. "I agree with you, my lord. I highly doubt he will come all the way from Lockwood to protect someone as inconsequential as her. He must have felt responsible for referring her name to us. He protects innocents like us from criminals like her."

"I concur," Lord Adair murmured from the doorway. "Since our fathers were such old friends, I thought it only fair to find out the truth myself."

Chapter Five

Lucy

Lucy dawdled on the doorstep, hoping Lord Adair would fetch her soon. Instead, the butler appeared in front of her, grabbed her arm and began dragging her inside the manor.

"You are hurting me," she snapped.

The butler's handsome face twisted, his lips stretched into a nasty smile, and his green eyes glittered like two pieces of rough, mismatched peridots. He looked, for a moment, like one of those painted masks one saw at the playhouse.

"This way," he said, with an odd high-pitched giggle. "Lord Adair has asked everyone to assemble in the formal drawing-room. That includes the servants."

"I am not a servant," she began struggling in his grip, her movements becoming frantic and desperate when he refused to loosen his hold.

He twisted her arm behind her back, and she felt his hot breath on her neck. She opened her mouth to scream only to find herself suddenly free.

She whirled around and gasped.

The butler was standing straight and stiff like a frozen statue. His eyes were bulging as if he had happened to gaze upon Medusa, while behind him stood Lord Adair holding the butler's neck in a casual grip.

"I learned a trick when I visited the royal family in the far east," Lord Adair said conversationally. "If I apply some pressure here," he poked the butler's nape, "it paralyses the person, and this spot, next to it, will kill him."

Lucy stood on her toes and arched her neck. "Which spot?"

Lord Adair released the butler, who dropped to his knees and clutched his head. "You will suffer a headache for a day or two," he remarked. "Next time, I see you misbehaving with a woman, lady or not, I will not be so considerate."

"How did you do that?" she asked again. "I couldn't see."

He ignored her question, his eyes on the red bands on her arm. "That is going to bruise, Miss Trotter."

She glanced at her arm and shrugged. "Eh, I have had worse." She bounced on her toes and asked, "Does pressing a small spot on the neck truly kill a man? Will you tell me where it is? Do you think I can do it? Does it take a lot of pressure or only a touch?"

"I suggest you refrain from such talk, considering you stand accused of murder."

Lucy closed her mouth and meekly shuffled after him.

The formal drawing room was an explosion of Pomona green and Spanish brown. The windows were small, the ceilings high, and the fireplace freshly lit. The room was cold and reeking of tea leaves that had been recently scattered to refresh the pale green carpet.

Lord Adair led her to a chair next to the fireplace. "Sit, Miss Trotter," he commanded.

And no one in the room dared to object as she sat in what was clearly the most coveted seat.

She stifled a sigh as the heat from the roaring fire warmed her bones. She allowed herself a moment of rest before looking around the room.

Lady Willoughby had draped herself on the overstuffed green sofa, her pink silk robe parted boldly at her ankles. On the other side of the sofa sat Jane, who was trying to either strangle a periwinkle cushion on her lap or disappear into its stuffing.

Lord Claybrook and Lord Willoughby sat on the chaise

longue, the arrangement clearly irking them both. They sat straight and stiff, shoulders and boots turned away from one another.

The valet swooped in just then, carrying a chair with Lord Aston perched upon it like an old, bony bird who had lost a good bit of its feathers. His frail body seemed almost childlike nestled in the large wooden chair.

Lucy admired the rings glinting on the old man's fingers. A sparkly emerald on his fourth hairy finger particularly captured her fancy.

The servants stood in a neat line near the doorway, wringing hands and mopping brows. The setting sun bathed them in an eerie orange glow. It all seemed surreal, like a play come to life.

Lucy smiled at them, and they promptly looked away, terrified. She rolled her eyes. She was hardly going to jump up, brandish the fire poker and stab them all to death.

Lord Adair took his place in front of the room. The soft glow from the sun shot through the window and landed on his face. He smiled, looking so handsome as to be unearthly.

The maids swooned.

The valet absently pulled off his boot and stuck his foot, clad in a holey sock, under their noses. They revived expeditiously.

Lucy dug her nails into the seat and focused on the flickering fire. She suddenly felt as if someone was squeezing her neck, allowing only a measured amount of air to trickle into her lungs.

Someone coughed in the room and skirts rustled.

This was it. She was about to learn if Lord Adair was going to throw her to the wolves or not.

"Thank you for capturing her," Lord Willoughby broke the silence. "We will inform the duke."

"I didn't capture her. She came to me seeking justice," Lord Adair corrected him.

Lady Willoughby frowned, "But surely you don't believe her. She must have done it. Who else could it be?"

"Do you have any proof?" Lord Adair asked.

"Someone was murdered in the house she had previously

worked in," Lord Claybrook said.

"A coincidence. She was entirely innocent, and the murderer was caught."

"Are you certain?"

"Are you suggesting that *I* apprehended the wrong man?"

Lord Claybrook looked away.

Lady Willoughby angled her body towards Lord Adair, letting a touch more of her ankle show. "She ran the moment we accused her."

"Perhaps, she knew no one would believe her. It is convenient to blame the outsider."

Lord Willoughby blinked. "You do not mean to say that . . . one of us did it?"

Lord Adair clasped his hands and remained silent.

"Are you suggesting we investigate this matter?" Lord Aston's thin, reedy voice came from the chair.

"It would be for the best."

"An investigation in Gopshall Manor?" Lord Aston asked again, his voice deepening in anger. "I will never allow it."

"Father is right," Lord Willoughby nodded at Lord Aston. "If word got out . . . It would be a scandal."

Lord Adair shrugged. "Lord Willoughby, the family suspects the bullet was meant for you. If Miss Trotter is innocent and is sentenced to the gallows or shipped off to penal colonies, what good will it do? It will save your family from a scandal, but it might end up being the last decision you ever make because the person who tried to kill you will try again. Will you be able to sleep comfortably every night knowing someone was waiting to murder you at the next opportune moment?"

A deadly silence fell in the room.

The cook standing near the door started trembling, making the teacups dance on the tray. Amongst the clattering of china, a slow understanding swept the room that all of them were suspects.

Lucy felt as if a weight had lifted off her chest, and the air whooshed into her lungs. She breathed deeply and gratefully.

She eyed Lord Adair like he was the most wonderful creature on earth. Her eyes shone with warmth and gratitude. He was brilliant. Absolutely brilliant.

No one would stop the investigation now, otherwise they would appear guilty. Also, Lord Willoughby was the head of the household. It was in his best interest to see that the real culprit was caught.

"Jane Peyton," Lady Willoughby shrieked suddenly. "She must have done it."

Lord Adair flicked a glance towards the girl sitting in the corner, her hands clasped together, her face pale and lips pinched.

"And what proof do you have?" Lord Claybrook snapped.

"She is too quiet," Lady Willoughby's voice shook. "She has been trying to seduce my husband. I know it. A woman knows these things."

Jane stared at Lady Willoughby in shock and betrayal.

"She is innocent. We were in the library together, writing letters when the murder occurred. We told you," Lucy spoke up. "But none of you believed us."

Tears shimmered in Jane's eyes, and a hint of guilt flashed across her face.

"She didn't try very hard to convince us," Lady Willoughby said spitefully. "Why, this morning she was ready to let Lucy take all the blame."

Jane's mouth hardened. "I did no such thing." Her soft voice was firm, a whisper spoken in a refined, ladylike manner that cut through Lady Willoughby's crass tone like butter.

"Would you like me to investigate the matter?" Lord Adair asked Lord Willoughby.

Lord Willoughby's eyes darted to his wife and away. "I would be grateful for your help."

Lord Adair smiled, and the women gasped. It wasn't every day that one saw the most handsome man in England smile. They squirrelled away the moment like a precious nugget to be dwelled upon in darker times, while Rosie, the maid, momentarily lost her mind and purred and barked for a bit.

Lord Adair dismissed them all except Lord Claybrook. "A word."

Lucy slipped out of the room, along with the family. She lingered near the door, wondering what Lord Adair wanted to speak to Claybrook about.

"Miss Trotter," Lord Adair stuck his head out from behind the door and narrowed his eyes.

"I was just leaving," she muttered. "I had dropped my reticule."

"Indeed."

She scowled and slinked away. A little bit of eavesdropping hurt no one.

Her steps slowed as she made her way towards her old bed chamber. Was it still hers? Had the servants thrown out her things? She didn't know where she stood anymore. Would the family toss her out and insist she find another place to live? Where would she go?

∞∞∞

Lucy was surprised to find Jane waiting for her in the hallway.

She grabbed her hand and squeezed. "Thank you."

Lucy was too worried to smile back. Her usual happy demeanour had been snowed upon. "I only spoke the truth."

"I tried to tell them that you were innocent."

"I know you did, but who believes the likes of us?"

Their rooms were next to each other, and they walked towards them in silence.

A thin wall divided their rooms, and if Lucy held her breath, she could sometimes hear Jane pottering about next door.

Lucy coughed, feeling oddly hot.

Jane paused outside Lucy's room, "You look unwell."

"I think I am going to lie down for a while."

"Can I get you some tea?"

Lucy shook her head. Another cough tickled the back of her

throat, and she hurried inside and closed the door behind her.

Despite staying next to each other for months, she and Jane had failed to become friends. She knew Jane saw her as a wild, untameable creature, someone she couldn't trust, while Lucy thought her too quiet and reserved and full of secrets.

The only thing the two girls were certain of was the fact that neither of them had murdered Lord Beazley, since they had happened to be together at the time.

Unless the family doctor had got the time of death wrong.

Jane could have done it. She could see the mouse-like girl planning the entire thing and fooling them all.

She paused at the thought, her heart suddenly beating fast. She slid an eye towards the wall, wondering if Jane stood behind it with a butcher's knife in hand, singing a lullaby and grinning like a loon?

She decided to speak to Lord Adair and ascertain the time of death as soon as possible.

Meanwhile, she crawled into her small, hard bed, pulled a thin woollen blanket over her head and closed her eyes. She felt horrible, but a good rest would set her right.

As for Jane, if she walked in with a cleaver and chopped her to pieces, Lord Adair would avenge her death . . . or so she hoped.

Chapter Six

Jane

"Come in," Lord Claybrook's deep voice washed over Jane like a bowl full of sunshine.

She smoothed her grey skirt and gripped the door handle. Her heart was pounding, and her face felt hot. She took a deep breath and walked into the study.

Lord Claybrook sat at the desk, reading a letter.

It was a small room with rosewood panels, maroon leather chairs, bookshelves and a cluttered desk. The carpet was cream and brown, and the scent of tobacco had sunk deep into its woollen pile.

She stood near the door, her eyes lingering on Claybrook's bent head. As she watched, a strand of dark hair fell forward on his forehead, and she instinctively stepped forward, worried it would end up in his eye.

He looked up then, and she dropped her eyes, bowed her head and curtsied.

"Sit," he ordered impatiently.

She sat.

"Lord Adair has asked me to interview everyone. He thinks the family will be more forthcoming if I asked the questions."

Jane didn't know how to reply. He didn't need to give her any explanations; after all, he was her employer. He had every right to question her. She clasped her hands and remained silent.

He threw the pen down, leaned back in his chair, and his eyes focused on her face. "How have the children taken the news?"

Jane's lips twitched. "They are delighted. They think nothing could be more exciting than a murder. Master Claybrook has already begun searching for clues, while Miss Claybrook took to her room this morning insisting, she was too delicate for such things. After a short nap, she decided it was better to be brave and help solve the crime than sit in her room, twiddling her thumbs."

He flashed a rare smile. "Hard to believe little Hannah playing the delicate maiden. She is a ruffian like her mother was."

She felt a dash of envy for the dead woman. To be so fondly remembered, even after her death so long ago, was something precious.

"What did you want to ask me?" she spoke a little more sharply than she intended.

He gestured towards the silver coffee pot.

She poured him a cup.

He steepled his fingers together and asked, "Your name is Jane Aubrey Peyton?"

She nodded; her fingers flew to her neck as she waited for his next question.

His eyes flickered to where her hand fluttered on pale, delicate skin. "Your father was a baron, and he lost his wealth when you were very young?"

She swallowed. He had already asked her these questions when he had hired her a year ago. Why repeat them now? "Yes. I was five when I lost my mother, and my father began neglecting his affairs. He c-could give us an education but nothing more than that."

"No dowry?"

"Nay."

"How many siblings do you have?"

"Three. One brother and two sisters."

"The property is entailed to your brother; I understand he is not very kind?"

"Yes, which is why I had to look for a post as did my sisters."

"What do your sisters do?"

"They are teachers in a school near my home in Winshire. I had to look for work farther afield since nothing was available for me. I did a bit of sewing for the village and helped the village doctor before I applied for this post."

He threw the quill down and walked towards the window. "It's a warm day. The snow is finally melting."

Jane frowned at the sudden change in topic.

He turned to look at her, his eyes blue as the sky outside. He had a curious expression on his face.

"Is there anything you would like to tell me, Jane? Divulge any hidden secrets?"

She lost her composure, hearing her name on his lips. He had never called her Jane before.

Perhaps, it was a mistake? He didn't seem to realise he had said it.

The scent of fresh coffee teased her nostrils, and she wished she could reach out and have a cup to moisten her dry throat.

He raised his brow. "Any secrets, Miss Peyton."

Her heart began beating hard and fast. His tone was layered. Almost coaxing, inviting confidences. Slowly, she shook her head.

He looked curiously unhappy and disappointed.

"I have nothing more to ask at the moment," he said, turning his back on her.

She hesitated, a question hovering on her lips. But, a knock on the door had her snap her teeth together and scuttle out.

She ran into Lucy outside.

"Miss Trotter! How are you?"

"Vexed."

"I meant your cough. I heard you barking away last night."

"I apologise for keeping you awake," she bristled. "I will try to neigh or moo the next time I feel the urge to cough. Would you prefer that?"

"I was worried," Jane soothed. "Can I do anything to help you feel better?"

Lucy looked taken aback. She stood gaping like no one had ever asked her such a thing before.

Jane eyed the girl worriedly. Her skin was pale, sweat glistened on her brow, and she looked even more slight and fragile than usual. She wanted to tuck her into bed and feed her until she was her lively self again. She said gently, "I can make you a warm posset or a cup of tea?"

Lucy's eyes widened even more. "I – Oh, I don't know what to say. I—Thank you, but I am fine. Truly."

"You can barely speak," she scolded. "I think you should go to your room and rest. I will take care of the children today."

"I have been asked to come here," Lucy rasped. "Claybrook wants to interview me when *I* should be the one interviewing *him*. I solved a murder, did you know? I did a fine job the last time."

"You want to investigate?" Jane asked incredulously.

"The lot of them are empty-headed fools. I am the only one with any experience in such matters. Besides, it is in our best interest to investigate, or we will be known as the infamous murdering governesses, and people will throw rocks at our heads when we walk towards the noose."

"Whatever do you mean, Miss Trotter?"

"They will think we killed him together."

"They will do no such thing!"

"The two of us are the only newcomers in Gopshall, and we announce that we were together at the time of the murder. Most dimwits would assume we killed Beastly Beazley, and the people in this mansion are exactly that. Dimwits."

"Hush, don't speak ill of the dead."

"He was beastly. He tried to bed you!"

Jane stilled. "You know?"

"Yes, I know. Claybrook punched him when he found him trying to accost you in the hallway."

"Oh, Lucy, does everyone know?"

Lucy's face softened. "No, I was right behind you. You were so distressed that you didn't notice me."

"What else did you see?"

"Beazley lay slumped in the corner, and I wanted to kick him as well . . . but I refrained. I saw him get up and follow Claybrook and you ran after them. Just then Master Willoughby came racing around the corner carrying two puddings and ran smack into me. I had to run back into my room to change. That child will be the death of me—"

Jane let Lucy ramble on, while her own thoughts lay in tangles. She recalled the evening when Beazley had accosted her and Claybrook had swooped in like a knight, punched the man and saved her honour. After that, Claybrook had stormed off to the library with Beazley at his heels. Beazley had demanded to know why he had hit him. Claybrook, in turn, had threatened him with a lot more if he so much as looked at Jane again.

She had felt curiously warm, hearing his low, menacing threat. The argument had escalated, and she had quietly slipped away.

Now, thinking back, she wondered how bad things had gotten that evening. How much had Beazley angered Claybrook? Enough to kill him?

After all, the argument had occurred the evening before he died.

She knew Claybrook was kind, warm and an excellent employer until someone tried taking advantage of him.

She knew he could turn brutal in a blink of an eye. He detested being lied to, and everyone back at Claybrook's home in Hartford knew not to upset him.

She clutched the hat stand as a wave of homesickness overcame her. Nostalgia, not for the house she grew up in, but for Hartford, Claybrook's residence.

She wished the children's grandfather had never requested their presence here at Gopshall Manor.

She wanted to eat Mary's meat pies again, go for a stroll by the seaside near their home, use the luxurious lavender and vetiver soaps that the housekeeper made in the kitchens. Even her room had been far more comfortable with big windows and proper curtains.

She reluctantly released the hat stand and headed towards the nursery. It was time to give the children a spot of tea.

She wondered what would happen to the children if Claybrook turned out to be the murderer. She bit her lip, feeling sick in the stomach.

They wouldn't suspect him if she kept the incident to herself. She would have to ask Lucy to keep it hidden too.

She wondered if the girl would oblige. If not … she might have to do something drastic to get her to keep her mouth shut.

Chapter Seven

Lucy

Lord Erasmus Gilbert Willoughby, the Earl of Aston, was sitting in the dining room drinking tea and wearing only his unmentionables.

Lucy was used to the sight by now. She had learned over the months that Lord Aston liked to dine in his unmentionables and nothing else; hence, the dining room was always kept unbearably warm.

She was glad she had been asked to eat in her rooms for she couldn't imagine eating a large meal in the dining room while sweating like a furry fox on a hot summer's day. It was also why Lady Willoughby was unable to have dinner parties, since an old man clad, in a brown unmentionable, flaunting old bones and bits of hair was bound to kill appetites.

Lucy curtsied to Lord Aston's bare right arm, which looked like a part of a thousand-year-old corpse she had once seen at the museum of curiosities, and quickly turned towards Lord Adair.

The vision of Lord Adair, clad in a beautiful blue silk robe, soothed her eyes like a luxurious eyewash. She let her eyes skim over his attractive figure, thinking this must be what the ladies felt when they dowsed their eyes with those fancy drops called Moonshine or Morning Dewdrops.

She wondered if he was wearing anything underneath the

robe. Her face flamed at the thought, yet, she couldn't tear her eyes away from him.

Would he mind terribly if she nibbled his ear?

"Miss Trotter?" Lord Aston thundered. "Stop ogling the man. What do you want?"

"A word with Lord Adair please," she replied meekly. She wasn't ashamed to be caught staring. Everyone stared at Lord Adair. It was impossible not to.

Lord Aston flicked his fingers in dismissal, and Lord Adair rose swiftly, caught her arm and hurried out of the room.

"Thank you. You saved me from melting into a puddle."

"You do look hot . . . a bit warm. Flushed." She bit her lip.

His eyes twinkled as he looked down at her, "A stroll should cool me down. The sun is out, but the sharp spring air should be pleasant enough."

Lucy didn't care if the spring air was sharp or blunt as long as Lord Adair was by her side. Everything seemed wonderful and safe when he was with her.

"How are you feeling?" he asked, as she rummaged around the coatroom for her thingamajigs.

She glanced up in surprise. "I feel fine."

"Truly?"

She looked away, and furiously rammed a hat on her head and began struggling with the gloves. No one had ever asked after her wellbeing before, whereas today she had been asked twice!

"Lucy," he chided gently. "Fix your coat, and that hat couldn't be yours."

She pulled off the dark brown fur hat and stared at it for a moment. "Looks like a cat I once knew." Instead, she retrieved a fruit-laden bonnet from the stand and put it on.

He seemed pained at the sight of the wobbling fruits crafted from old socks adorning her hat.

She ignored his expression and strode out the door. She happened to like her hat. It had taken her months to make it. She was particularly proud of the pear dangling near her ear since it looked almost real in certain lights.

They walked quickly and in companionable silence, and once they were a fair distance from the house, she turned towards him,

"Why did you ask Lord Claybrook to question the guests? Why didn't you ask me? I solved the case at Rudhall. Surely, I should be assisting you?"

"You are like a tenacious bee. You were bound to fly into the face of truth at Rudhall at some point. As for Lord Claybrook, he is sensible, intelligent and understands the family. He knows what questions to ask and where to prod. He will procure the answers faster than I can."

"No one can be quicker than you in getting to the truth of the matter," she said with conviction.

"Why thank you, my dear, but I can only do so much. I have to go to London on an urgent matter, and while I am gone, I have requested Claybrook to be in charge."

"I can be your assistant. I have experience."

"Can you imagine Lady Willoughby answering your questions?"

"But I can help in other ways. I am stealthy, intelligent, educated. I can play the piano, the harpsichord, the flute. I can write exquisite letters, speak French and argue like a Greek philosopher. I can knit, sort of sew, paint and dance. I can bake divine little cakes light as air—"

"Miss Trotter—"

"I know how to prise a bullet out of a man and make a salve for a nasty cut," she continued. "I know how to use the hunga munga, the lethal African fighting tool. I can brawl like an experienced street urchin."

"Here," He pulled out a long knife with a curved, ivory handle from his coat and handed it to her. "The first time we met, you had mentioned your skill with the hunga munga, and I just happened to come across the weapon in a pawn shop, so I procured it for you."

"Oh," she took it gingerly. "I-thank you. It's lovely. A fine specimen of the hunga munga."

"Now, I would like a demonstration."

"What?"

"Show me how to use it."

"Eh … well, the ground is a bit mushy. Not right for this sort of thing," she said, stamping around and sliding her foot from left to right and back again.

He took the weapon back and shook his head. "That is an ordinary, if an ornate knife, and not the hunga munga."

She gasped in outrage. "You tricked me!"

He stared at her coldly. "Do not lie to me again, Miss Trotter."

"I-I apologise." She dropped her eyes, feeling ashamed. She continued in a small voice. "You could teach me."

"I don't have the time to teach you."

"But I want to help. I can find the murderer quicker than Claybrook can. In fact, what if Claybrook is the murderer?"

"Could be," Lord Adair shrugged. "Time will tell."

"Everyone is a suspect?" she asked.

"Everyone, including you."

"And you will not let me assist you?"

"Nay. It is too dangerous."

Lucy scowled. Her neck was already on the way to the noose. Things could not get any more perilous than that.

She ran a hand over her face, feeling helpless.

She had to solve the case not because she did not have faith in Lord Adair's abilities, but because she wanted to prove to him that she was a worthy ally.

"My lord," she said, squaring her shoulders and facing him. "I know you see me as a damsel in distress, and I admit I have exaggerated my accomplishments a smidgeon—"

"Miss Trotter."

"—But I must assert that deep in my heart, I am a warrior waiting to hone my skills. A cold-blooded, intelligent woman, who has the capabilities to be an excellent spy …. Ack!" She tripped over a branch and landed on the muddy ground.

He stared down at her. "Skills, Miss Trotter?" he asked with a raised brow.

"Lawks!" She spat a glob of mud and glared at him. "You could have warned me, my lord."

"And taken away your chance to shine?"

Tears pricked her eyes. She had failed, yet, again. And if things continued the way they were going, she would never win his trust, he would never help her learn the art of investigation, and she would never discover her parents' whereabouts.

She furiously whacked the wet mud staining her bodice and skirts. He was the only one who could help her find answers to her questions. Who had written the anonymous letter that warned her that all she knew about the family was a *Banbury tale*? Why was she left in an orphanage? Did her parents die, or did they live with a brood of children far bigger than they could afford to feed . . . or worse, was she illegitimate?

She wanted to sink to her knees and beg him to help her.

He kept walking, swinging his cane, oblivious to her torment.

They walked deeper into the woods, and Gopshall was now completely hidden from view. The piles of leaves and pine needles soaked in melted snow squelched under her feet, while birds, somewhere high above, chirped a greeting.

She shivered as the trees with their new green leaves threw dappled shadows on the ground and stole some of the sun's warmth.

"At least, tell me all you have learned about the case," Lucy pleaded.

He turned to face her. His hair gently blew in the breeze, and she took a step back from him so she could concentrate on his words rather than his warm, luxurious scent and the pulsating heat emanating from him.

"Nothing I say will stop you from investigating will it?" he asked with a laugh.

She shook her head. He knew her too well.

He nodded. "I will tell you all I have learned, but after that, you are on your own. I am not going to be around to save you, Miss Trotter, so you will have to be careful."

"I promise. Now, quick tell me."

He sighed. "Lord Beazley had been visiting his ageing aunt in Truntlewood. It began snowing shortly after he departed, and the bad weather forced him to cut his journey short and instead of heading to London, he decided to spend a night at Gopshall. The weather continued to deteriorate, so he stayed another night eating, drinking and gambling with Lord Willoughby.

On the third morning of his stay, he was found dead by the valet deep in the woods behind the house. Somewhere here, as it so happens."

She eyed the dirt, the melting grey snow and the silent trees and felt her stomach lurch. No matter how many times she had seen death, it never ceased to frighten her.

He placed his hand on her arm. "As you know, the family assumed the shot was for Lord Willoughby since Lord Beazely was wearing Lord Willoughby's clothes, and they have a similar physique."

She pursed her lips thoughtfully. "His visit was a surprise; hence if he had any enemies, they wouldn't have known about it, and the storm kept outsiders at bay."

He turned back towards the house, his cane making puffs of snow as it hit the ground. His overcoat rippled behind him as he increased his speed.

She coughed and quickened her steps to keep up. "Lord Willoughby is not a nice man." Her throat burned as she spoke. "He often gets angry and throws things around in a fit of rage. He mistreats the servants, tries to paw the maids, his wife hates him, and Lord Claybrook detests him. In short, no one likes him, and everyone wants to do away with him."

He whacked his cane on the ground, silencing her. "My carriage should arrive soon," he said. "I will be off for a few days. Be good."

"One more question," she said. "Was the doctor right about the time of death? He said Lord Beazley died at eight in the morning or thereabouts."

"He is right."

"It couldn't possibly be two hours earlier?"

"No."

Her shoulders slumped in relief. "That means Jane is innocent. Thank goodness."

The sounds of horses' clip-clopping down the driveway reached them. A moment later, a dark carriage burst into view and thundered to a halt in front of them. Lord Adair's valet, Barnaby, leapt off the front seat that he had been sharing with the driver and handed over a letter.

Lord Adair read it, crumpled it in his fist and shoved it deep into his pocket. His jaw tensed and, for a moment, he looked vulnerable.

She was intrigued. What could possibly rattle someone like him?

He flung open the carriage door and placed a foot on the step. "I have to leave, Miss Trotter."

"Does your trip have anything to do with this case?"

His face darkened. "No."

She blinked at his expression, suddenly remembering who he was. She took a step back and curtsied to hide her face.

Perhaps, one day, he would tell her his secrets and allow her to help him.

When she looked up again, it was to find him rolling away in the carriage leaving behind a trail of swirling dust, ice and wind.

He had left her alone to face a nest of vipers.

Chapter Eight

Jane

Jane dipped a strip of cloth in a bowl of water and wiped Lucy's brow.

Lucy opened her eyes and blinked in confusion. "Gack?"

"The physician is on the way."

"Truglee?"

Jane put the cloth on the table and helped Lucy sit up. "I suspect you were ill last night. When you did not wake at your usual hour, I came to check on you and found you delirious with fever."

Lucy looked away and pulled the sheet up to her chest. "Did I say anything while I was ... not in my senses?"

"You believed I was your pet raven."

"Spinoza?"

"You told me to keep my beak straight, not peck the fruit cake and scolded me for frightening the sparrows."

"Anything else?"

"You asked me to find a Mrs Raven."

"I see."

"And have little baby ravens."

"Oh."

"You wanted to be a grandmother before they hung you."

"Before who hanged me?"

"You didn't specify."

A dash of awkwardness scurried in along with the gentle breeze from the slash in the wall that was the window.

She shifted in her seat, desperately trying to think of some mundane topic. She finally asked, "How are you feeling?"

"Better," Lucy croaked. "I appreciate your concern."

"I am glad I was able to help." She watched Lucy run a finger around her collar, which she guessed was sticky with sweat. "Would you like to wash?"

Lucy brightened. "Yes, please."

She stood up and held out her hand.

Lucy frowned in confusion.

"I will help you to the washstand," she explained.

Lucy shook her head. "Ah, I . . . can manage."

Jane nodded briskly. "I am going to bring you something to eat and a cup of tea. I suggest you stay in your room for the rest of the day."

Lucy blinked back owlishly. Some colour had returned to her cheeks, and her eyes were alert allaying some of Jane's concern.

She left the room and headed to the kitchen, feeling sorry for the girl.

∞∞∞

"Get back into bed," Jane said, from the doorway.

"I have much to do," Lucy argued. She had changed into a morning gown and was now battling with a pair of stockings. Her toe was stuck in a hole where the thigh was meant to be.

"Post letters? Darn your socks? I will do it all. Meanwhile, glue yourself to the bed."

"I have to investigate."

"You need to heal; your throat sounds terrible."

"My throat has a lot more to worry about than a cold. It sounds croaky because it is terrified of the noose speeding towards it."

"You cannot ask questions if you have no voice," she snapped.

"Get into bed and have some breakfast."

"I am not eating your breakfast."

"This is not mine, it's yours," she lied smoothly.

"The cook hates me. She would never make up a tray for me."

"I told her you were on your deathbed and your last wish was to have a good breakfast. She was eager to oblige."

"Oh," Lucy took the tray and sat down. "Thank you."

Jane nodded and sat on the chair by the desk. Her fingers drummed the table as she watched the girl eat. Her own stomach growled, but she ignored it.

They didn't speak much; the tension was thick and sticky in the air like honey on skin.

She was worried about the way Lucy had unpeeled herself from the bed and was ready to dive into the investigation. The girl needed to rest, but her refusal meant that she was not only obstinate but also foolish. She wished she could grab the pillow and whack her on the head a few times to make her see sense.

Lucy drained the teacup and said, "You didn't do it."

Jane frowned. "Didn't do what?"

"Kill Beastly Beazley."

Jane stared at Lucy. She had always suspected the woman to be mad. Brave, but decidedly loony. "I don't understand."

"I let you think that I trusted you when, in fact, I didn't."

Jane blinked at that. "I was with you when the murder occurred."

"I know, but that would only be true if the village doctor had been honest about the timing of the death."

"Why would he tell a Banbury tale?"

Lucy leaned back on the pillow and tucked her booted feet under the blanket. "What if you and the village doctor were having a secret liaison and he changed the time to protect you?"

"Eh? He must be a hundred years old!"

"Or the two of you are part of a criminal gang."

"Are not!"

"Or a maggoty brained father and daughter who kill, rob and then flee from village to village to escape conviction?"

Jane sprang up in outrage. "How dare you?"

"You could have killed Beazley, strolled home and then pretended that you were with me the entire time. And the doctor would have pronounced the man dead much later than the hour he actually died to save you."

She couldn't believe she had spent the entire morning nursing this awful girl. She leapt off the chair and charged out of the room, blind with rage.

Lucy followed her, "But Adair assured me that the man died when we were together, so you are innocent. The doctor's verdict can be trusted."

Jane stopped abruptly, spun on her heels and examined the girl.

Bits of thread had escaped Lucy's collar and cuffs. The hem wasn't sewn straight, but her bright eyes, soft mouth and thick, silky brown hair made up for her lack of sewing skills. She looked like a starved, apologetic rabbit and Jane thawed, feeling her lips twitch in amusement.

"Suspect everyone," Lucy explained hurriedly. "It's something I learnt while solving the Rudhall case."

She burst into laughter. "You are absurd . . . your imagination is wild, like your locks. All those scenarios .... It didn't even cross my mind."

Lucy patted her shoulder. "That sort of thinking comes with experience and a bloodthirsty soul."

A throat cleared behind them, making them leap and twist like dancers.

They found Lord Claybrook leaning against the doorway of the dining room.

Jane swallowed nervously and took a step back. She was surprised they had walked this far so quickly. Anger and inane chatter, it seemed, hastened time.

He straightened his back, his eyes pinned on her face. His broad shoulders took up most of the hallway, dwarfing the space instantly.

He turned towards them, blocking the light streaming in

from the window, and plunging his face into shadow.

She felt her heart skip, while her eyes raced over every bit of him. She noticed the dark tinge under his eyes and the faint lines around his mouth.

Lucy dipped into a curtsy, nudging her to do the same.

"Miss Trotter," Lord Claybrook nodded in greeting. "Will you kindly bring your bloodthirsty soul for an interview again in the study?"

Jane tripped on air.

Lucy steadied her, "I will, my lord."

"I thought you already interviewed her," Jane stuttered.

Claybrook wrinkled his nose. "We were about to begin, but Miss Trotter spotted a bee. Did you know she is deathly afraid of bees? She ran out of the room, screaming like a tortured cat."

Lucy dipped her head, "It's spring. The bees are everywhere."

"I will keep the windows closed this time and see you in my study at noon. Until then, please retire to your room and feign illness since the physician is on his way to see you. I don't want him to feel as if he has wasted valuable time by coming here."

Jane watched Lucy fly back to her room, a smile hovering on her lips. Bees indeed. It was never dull with Miss Lucy Trotter around.

She looked back at Claybrook and found him staring at her. Her smile died.

She cleared her throat and squeaked, "I am just heading to the nursery."

He didn't respond, his eyes glued to her face.

She patted her hair and discreetly checked her teeth. "My lord?"

"Yes?"

"You are . . . staring. Do I have anything on my face?"

"It's perfect."

"Oh." She took a step towards him.

He cocked his head and raised a brow.

"You are still staring at me, and you are in my way."

"I apologise, I feel a little muddled this morning." He stepped aside and gestured for her to go ahead.

She began walking down the hallway while he strolled next to her, seemingly in no hurry.

He spoke now, "Some of the household staff, along with William . . . I mean, Lord Willoughby, searched the grounds. They found no footprints. Curious."

She was surprised he was sharing the information with her. Did that mean he trusted her? The thought pleased her, and she ducked her head to hide her blush.

She was finding it a little challenging to be around him these days. At the same time, she looked forward to seeing him all day. This conflicting feeling was very odd and distressing.

She frowned, was Lucy's madness catching? What was wrong with her? She quickened her steps to get away from him.

She bit her lip when he turned left at the end of the hallway. "Did you want to visit the children?"

"I did and to see you safe in the nursery. You have started stumbling a lot more since we arrived at Gopshall."

Jane tripped on air …again.

He reached out, caught her arm and swung her around to face him.

Everything went silent.

Her ears filled with air and his face filled her vision. She took a sharp unsteady breath in a futile attempt to calm her racing heart.

The warmth of his fingers seeped into her arm, and her chest rose and fell in agitation.

"Are you listening?" he asked, stroking a thumb across her skin.

Her mind clouded, and she could think of nothing else but his fingers on her bare skin.

A soft gasp escaped her, and his eyes narrowed and dropped to her lips.

He pulled her closer, and her stomach clenched.

She tried to school her features, tried to hide the turmoil raging inside her. It was becoming difficult to breathe, as if the air around her was slowly turning solid. She felt like swooning, and a part of her wished she would so his effect on her could remain a secret.

His voice was gentle, unlike the intensity in his eyes. "Is something the matter? I know it's not as pleasant here as my home, but surely that couldn't be the reason for your sudden clumsiness."

His words protruded the fog in her brain, and she desperately tried to make sense of it.

She spoke without thinking, "You—"

"I?" His sharp voice brought her back to her senses.

She stepped away from him. "I mean the murder—"

He shook his head and began walking once more. "You were acting oddly before the murder occurred. I had meant to have a word with you about that, but what with recent events I—" He paused, searching her face. "You were always so sure on your feet. I have seen you race up the hill, hop over puddles, skip over rocks as expertly as an agile goat."

She flushed and dropped her lashes. She didn't know if she should be vexed at being compared to a goat or pleased at how much he had noticed her.

She quickened her steps, forcing her eyes to focus on the paintings on the wall rather than the man walking beside her.

His tone suddenly became concerned. "It's not your health, is it? Should I call a physician? I know taking care of the children is hard work, and if it is too much for you, you can go home after the murder is solved, for a short while. You haven't seen your family in a long time."

She stiffened. "Its very kind of you to think of me, my lord, but I am fine. I apologise for my clumsiness. I will make sure it doesn't happen again. I can take care of the children."

"You misunderstand me, Miss Peyton. I—"

"Father!" the children squealed, and she was grateful for the interruption. She headed to the cupboard in the nursery and pretended to tidy the clothes while Lord Claybrook hugged his two children: love and affection evident on his face.

She looked away from the sight feeling like an intruder. She was a servant and no more. She always had to remember her place. She took a deep breath to steady her limbs and forced herself to focus on the task at hand and not the man laughing a few feet away from her.

One of these days she was going to forget herself and do something foolish. She closed her eyes and let a tear escape. She would have to find a new position as soon as the murderer was found.

Chapter Nine

Lucy

Lord Claybrook tapped the silver snuff box with the back of his quill. "It's curious isn't it that you have been employed twice and both times a murder happened to occur in your employers' homes."

Lucy straightened her back. "It does seem like a remarkable coincidence, but I assure you, that's all it is."

"You grew up in an orphanage?"

"The Brooding Cranesbill. About four days journey from here."

He nodded and swiftly wrote it down.

"Lots of children died at the orphanage," she said. "Surely, you don't think I killed them as well?"

"I am not making any judgements, Miss Trotter. I am asking questions and reporting my answers to Lord Adair. He can deduce what he pleases from them. Now, do you enjoy being a governess?"

"It's a privilege to get such a post," she hedged.

"Do you get angry a lot, Miss Trotter?"

"I could say I have the temperament of a Persian cat or a bloodhound. I could even say I am as dull as a turtle. You wouldn't know the truth, since you cannot read my mind. I doubt a murdering creature would be very honest about such things."

"Answer the question."

"If someone took the time to take a gun, follow Lord Beazley, wait for him to get far away from the manor and then shoot him in the back, then it clearly means it was planned and not a momentary lapse of senses. Some cold-blooded creature, I think—"

"Enough."

She leaned forward in her seat. "Did you know Lord Beazley well, my lord?"

"No," he scowled. "He was a mere acquaintance."

"Did you like him?"

"No."

"Do you like your brother?"

He shot her a sharp look. "*I am* supposed to be the one asking the questions, Miss Trotter. Kindly answer them."

Lucy cast her eyes down and said meekly, "Yes, my lord."

He dipped his quill in ink when she spoke again. "You should ask me about my relationship with each member of the household."

"I will ask you what I want, when I want, and how I want. Is that clear?"

She jerked upright in her chair. "What if Beazley was a traitor to the king and Adair sent me to kill him?"

"Did he send you to kill him?"

"No, but you shouldn't take my word for it."

Lord Claybrook pinched the bridge of his nose and smeared ink all over it.

"Is something the matter, my lord? Does your headache terribly? Oh, you haven't been poisoned, have you? I will be done for if they find me in the room with a fresh corpse."

"Miss Trotter, for the next ten minutes, answer my questions and refrain from doing anything else but giving me short, simple and honest answers."

She sat back down. "Can I have some tea?"

"Drink the damn pot dry," he cursed.

She carefully poured them both a cup and sipped. "I *could* drink the pot dry. This is a lovely tea. It has a flowery aroma with tart undertones. Jasmine? Not something I would like at breakfast, mind, but pleasant enough. Please continue. I am ready to answer your questions."

"You need to remember your place," he snapped.

She handed him a handkerchief. "You have a spot of ink on your nose, my lord. It seems you have a short temper. Which means that you could have shot him in a fit of rage .... But then you are an intelligent man, and we agreed it was premeditated —"

He shot to his feet; his eyes narrowed to pinpricks. "Eat the sandwiches, drink the tea for as long as you like. I am going for a walk. I don't need to interview you, since Lord Adair knows you well enough. If he has any more questions, he can ask you himself. Good afternoon."

The door banged shut, and she waited for his footsteps to recede before grinning from ear to ear. It was a small victory, but victory, nonetheless.

Now, it was time she began her own investigation. She pulled a piece of parchment towards herself and picked up the abandoned quill.

She squinted at the paper and tapped her lips, where to begin?

Chapter Ten

Jane

Jane set her quill down, her heart thundering. The clock had struck two a few moments ago; surely, no one could be awake at this hour. And yet, she had heard a soft scrape of a boot outside her door.

There it was again. A soft step and a stifled sneeze. She extinguished the candle and went to the door and stuck her ear to the wood.

Another sneeze! Louder this time.

What if it was the killer prowling outside? What if he caught her?

Her hand flew to her mouth in horror. What if he was looking for a new victim?

A steadying breath later, a new thought bloomed in her mind. This was her chance to discover more and mayhap find the killer, save her skin and perhaps Claybrook's too.

She took a deep breath and forced herself to calm down and think. If it were the murderer, then he would kill her, or she would hang later anyway since everyone thought she and Lucy had killed Beazley.

It was a choice between dying now or later.

Did the noose hurt more or a gunshot to the head?

She needed to be brave and discover more. She had to set her fears aside and fight to survive. She would not walk to the slaughterhouse like a meek lamb. She would fight every inch of the way.

She was a tigress waiting to roar, an elephant tossing her trunk in defiance, a beautiful swan madly flapping her wings to defend herself.

She felt a surge of excitement and courage rush through her, and her ancestors danced in glee as she readied for battle.

She straightened her spine, tossed her braid behind her back, gripped the door handle and opened the door.

She allowed an eyeball to inch out of the room and spotted a grey figure holding a candle hurtling around the corner.

A deep breath later, she sped after the figure.

"Beazley, here Beazley. Where are you?"

Jane skidded to a halt as Lucy's voice floated over to her.

"Aunt Sedley, can you send Beazley down?"

Jane's mouth dropped open in shock, and her skin pebbled in the cold. The poor girl had gone mad. She was calling a dead man.

She padded towards the window and found Lucy staring at a broken, empty chair with her candle held aloft.

The pale glow of the candle illuminated Lucy's brown hair which fell in wild waves around her face. Her dull woollen dress hung from her shoulders, too big for her fragile figure. Her skin was pale and sweat beaded her forehead. Her eyes, though, were clear, bright and intelligent. They didn't show a hint of madness.

"Beazley! Don't you want justice? Come out now!" Lucy hissed.

Jane heard another footstep, this time, behind herself. Perhaps, a servant had woken and come to investigate?

She sprang towards Lucy, clamped a hand over the girl's mouth and whispered in her ear, "Shh. Someone is coming. We need to hide."

Lucy promptly pinched the tallow candle and dowsed them in darkness. The acrid smell of burning fat and smoke filled the air.

Jane dropped her fingers from Lucy's mouth and gripped her hand instead.

Lucy squeezed back in understanding, and they slipped behind the curtains.

Footsteps became louder and stopped right where they stood. Just a length of blue fabric separated them from the person, and the girls clung to each other in terror.

After a few moments, the footsteps receded, and Jane flung aside the curtains and ran towards her room.

Her courage bounced off to greener pastures, leaving her wobbling like a blancmange.

Lucy was right behind her, and the two girls collapsed on the bed with a sigh of relief followed by a fit of hysterical giggles.

"Thank you for saving me," Lucy finally gasped.

"A moment." Jane fumbled in the dark until she found a candle and the tinder box.

The click clacking of flint striking steel filled the small room until a flame flared into life.

In the candlelight, the two girls eyed one another uneasily.

"I heard you talking," Jane cleared her throat, unsure of how to go one. How did one ask if the other was mad? She finally settled on, "Have you lost your marbles?"

Lucy's eyes widened. "You heard me?"

Jane swallowed nervously. "You were trying to talk to Beazley. He is …err… dead. Very dead. And everyone thinks we killed him."

Lucy turned bright red. "I know."

"I don't understand."

"And yet you saved me."

"I don't know why," she frowned. "I am feeling baffled right now. It's not a state that I am used to."

Lucy sat up on the bed and hugged the pillow. "You won't believe me."

"Nonetheless, I would like to hear an explanation."

"I will have to start from the beginning."

"I am listening."

"It's a long story."

"I am not sleepy."

"I don't think I should."

"I will tell Claybrook, and you will be off to Bedlam in the morning."

Lucy drew her legs to her chest and rested her chin on her knees. "I used to work as a governess in Rudhall Manor when I was accused of murdering Lord Sedley. While living there, I saw a ghost manifest one night. It was Aunt Sedley. Well, not my aunt but the family's aunt. I don't know why I call her aunt . . . Well, that's not important. What is important is that she was restless about her brother's murder. She helped me investigate. When I left the place, she came along with me to Lockwood, Lord Adair's home and met Lord Adair's great grandfather's ghost. They fell in love and moved on to the afterlife, or I hope she did."

"You *have* lost your marbles." Jane gasped.

"I know it sounds ridiculous, but it's true. Every time I felt Aunt Sedley manifest, I would feel a queer chill. Curtains would tremble, threads would dance, and my skin would pebble. Then tonight, I suddenly began shivering and wondered if it was Beazley. The chill was coming and going so I think he was trying to lead me somewhere. I walked down the hallway and realised that the spot where the broken chair sat was the coldest. I am certain Beazley was waiting for me, and he would have shown himself had you not popped up."

"You are talking nonsense. The fever has gone to your head."

"I assure you; I am as sane as you are."

"The chill you felt was due to your illness, and that corner was colder than the rest of the hallway because it has a window directly above it with a broken latch."

"Oh," Lucy's shoulders slumped. "I was hoping his ghost would come and tell us who killed him."

Jane was unsure of what to think. Lucy didn't look mad, and yet what she said sounded impossible.

"I don't blame you for doubting me," Lucy echoed her

thoughts. "I wouldn't believe me either."

"It would have been helpful to have Beazley announce his murderer to us," Jane mused. "I still don't know what to believe."

"Please don't tell Claybrook or I will be off to Bedlam."

"On one condition. Don't tell Adair about the fact that Claybrook and Beazley fought the night before the murder."

"I will not, but I wouldn't be surprised if Lord Adair already knows."

"Just keep it to yourself, Miss Trotter."

"I will. And call me Lucy. Promise, you will keep tonight's happening to yourself?"

"You are decidedly mad but, then, who is not? Everyone has a bit of madness in them. Your secret is safe."

"Thank you, Miss Peyton."

"Jane."

"Jane," Lucy yawned and stood up. "I had better go to bed. It's late. If Beazley wants to talk to me, then he can come to my room. I am not going to go hunting for him again."

"If you had been caught, the family would have become even more suspicious."

"I realise that now and will be careful, henceforth. I will see you in the morning." She moved towards the door but paused at the sight of a paper gleaming with ink lying on the desk.

In a trice, Jane leapt up, landed near the desk and placed her hand on the letter. The ink was still wet; she had forgotten to sand it. It would be smeared all over her palm now, but that couldn't be helped. She moved to block the letter entirely from view and turned towards Lucy with a strained smile.

Lucy smiled back and politely averted her eyes.

The moment Lucy left, Jane lit the letter on fire using the candle flame and then tossed the burning paper into a basin of water.

Chapter Eleven

Lucy

Lucy eyed the eggs, pound cake, bread and butter, warm toast, fruits, hot rolls, pots of tea, coffee and the small mountain of bonbons and frowned. Why had Lady Willoughby asked her and Jane to join the family for breakfast?

"Now that the roads are clear, we are sending the children away," Lady Willoughby set her fork down and sipped her tea. "We can't have a criminal minding our children."

Ah! So, they had meant to invite her for a meal, present her with all manner of delicious food, kick the chair from under her and laugh when she fell on her backside.

She narrowed her eyes. Lady Willoughby could play at being the queen, but she refused to be an obedient subject.

As for the fact that her charges were being sent off, she couldn't be more pleased. If Lady Willoughby thought she had grown attached to the children and would be sad to see them leave, then she couldn't be further from the truth.

She was delighted with the news. So much so, that it took all her will power to stay put in her seat rather than leap up on the table and dance with the butter and the spoons.

She flexed her fingers, curled them into a ball of defiance, "We didn't murder him. What motive could we have?"

"Both of you tried to seduce my husband, and when that didn't work, you decided to kill him."

Lucy stabbed a boiled egg and popped two bonbons in her mouth. She proceeded to pile her plate with grapes, lemon cake and bacon. She chewed quickly while the family watched her swallow mouthful after mouthful of food in the most unladylike manner.

Lord Willoughby enjoyed good food; hence, the table was always laid with the most exquisite dishes. The jams had speckled gold leaves swirled through it, the biscuits had been bought from the most exceptional baker in London and brought all the way to Gopshall. The meats were tender and juicy, and the chocolate bonbons were French and delicious.

She finally drained her teacup and leaned back in her chair with a sigh of contentment. She had eaten a delicious meal, and now if they dismissed her for speaking her mind, then it mattered not a jot.

"Lady Willoughby," she said, feeling wonderfully full and drowsy, "why in the world would we, the poor governesses, flirt with your husband? If we had to seduce anyone, it would be Lord Claybrook."

Lord Claybrook choked on his coffee.

Lucy ignored the shocked faces around her and continued, "He is far more handsome, wealthy, intelligent and has a better physique than your husband, don't you agree, Jane?"

Jane tried to disappear into her sewing basket, while Lord Claybrook blushed like a young debutante at her coming-out ball.

Lady Willoughby was struck speechless. She sipped her hot chocolate and seethed in silence. She finally spoke through clenched teeth, "If Lord Adair hadn't insisted we keep you here, I would have shown you the door for your impertinence."

Lucy bit into an apple and crunched loudly. She wouldn't have spoken her mind, but now that the children were leaving and Lord Adair had instructed the family to keep her in the house until the case was solved, she didn't see the point in being polite.

They had accused her of murdering Beazley without investigating the matter. They didn't care if she lived or died as a result, so why should she care about their affected upper-class feelings?

She was no retiring wallflower, and if they tried to stamp on her poor orphaned soul, then she had every intention of leaving a few bruises before they shipped her off to the penal colonies.

"John is refusing to go," Lord Willoughby whispered from the corner. His plate was untouched, which was rather odd.

"He is old enough to take care of himself," Lady Willoughby said absently. "He can stay. The rest leave after breakfast."

Lucy almost let slip a cry of frustration. The elder son of Lord Willoughby, John, was seven years old and the naughtiest creature she had ever met. If it hadn't been for him, she wouldn't have slipped on the deuced chicken and ended up in Lord Willoughby's arms and been blamed for the murder.

Lord Aston suddenly whistled like a steaming kettle.

She jumped in shock as did Jane and the rest of the family.

"Have you lost your marbles?" Lady Willoughby snapped at the guffawing old man.

Lord Aston pointed at Lord Willoughby, who had turned a peculiar shade of grey and snorted. "Haven't you noticed the terror that has crept into your cowardly husband's heart? The fact that someone is out to murder him has finally sunk into his dense brain. Look at him, mewling like a kitten. Oh, he has turned a pretty shade, hee hee."

"He is your son," Claybrook snapped. "Have a heart."

Lord Aston didn't respond since he was busy chuckling into his snuff handkerchief.

"Enough of this nonsense," Lady Willoughby tapped her fingertips in glee. "I have some more news to impart to the lovely ladies here. Lord Claybrook has decided to send his children away as well."

Jane's shocked face made Lady Willoughby purr in satisfaction.

Lucy was furious. Lord Claybrook should have broken the news to Jane in a delicate manner. To spring it upon the poor thing like that …. Why it was wicked!

She tilted her head and eyed Lady Willoughby in irritation. She knew why this sudden resentment for Jane had sprung forth in her heart like an eager daffodil in spring. Lady Willoughby had noticed Lord Claybrook's spirited defence of Jane the other day, and that had set the rusty wheels in her head spinning. She probably assumed that Jane was Lord Claybrook's mistress and was vexed.

Lord Claybrook looked uncomfortable. "I was going to tell you, Miss Peyton."

Jane stood up, her lips tight and her fists balled. She spoke through clenched teeth as if keeping some strong emotion at bay, "I should help the children pack."

Lucy watched Jane leave and began counting under her breath, "One, two, three—"

Lord Claybrook hopped up and sped after Jane.

Lady Willoughby's face was apoplectic, and Lucy ducked her head to hide her smile. Without meaning to, Jane in her quiet, dignified way was making Lady Willoughby extremely furious.

It was entertaining to watch.

"The roads have been cleared, and most of the ice has melted," Lord Willoughby whispered from the corner again. He was clad in a dark robe and was sweating profusely. He peered at the shadows, every now and then, like a trapped, well-fed rat with shiny red eyes.

Lucy felt sorry for the man. He *was* awful, but that didn't mean he deserved to die.

"Toot, toot!" Lord Aston screeched in his son's face.

Lord Willoughby leapt into the air and flapped like a terrified bat.

Lucy couldn't help but giggle at the sight. Apart from his dark robe, made from the same fabric as the dark blue curtains hanging in the dining room, he was carrying a gun, a dagger, and a bow and arrow.

She could see a large chunk of the curtain was missing and wondered who spent the night creating the eye-watering robe for him.

He had stayed quiet throughout breakfast and for such a large man, had done an excellent job of blending into the furnishings.

She turned her attention to Lord Aston, who was still cackling away. He continued to snicker and then suddenly with a *thunk* landed on his toast and went silent.

Had he keeled over and died?

The valet appeared behind the old man and poked and prodded him, then checked his pulse.

"He is asleep," the valet finally concluded.

"Take him to his room," Lady Willoughby shuddered. "And don't let him out."

Lucy chewed on a piece of dry toast and watched the family follow Lord Aston out. She lifted her hand and signalled Spinoza, her pet raven, who flew into the room from an open window and settled on her shoulder.

She stroked his feathers feeling contemplative. The murder had brought forth the madness in all of them it seemed.

Mortal fear often created an excellent atmosphere to study the psyche, she realised.

True, it was an excellent way to study the human mind and, yet, she couldn't present a few alarmed derrieres to a wild bear simply to ignite primitive survival skills for further experimentation.

She wiped her hand on the napkin and stuffed the handkerchief full of chocolate into her reticule along with an apple, and a slice of bread and butter.

She turned her mind to lighter matters and wondered how Lord Claybrook was smoothening Jane's ruffled feathers.

She looked the raven in the eye and said huskily, "I am becoming broody and philosophical, Spinoza," she whispered. "Hopefully, Lord Claybrook and Jane are having a rather more interesting time . . . I wonder if they are kissing?"

Chapter Twelve

Jane

Jane flew down the corridor towards the nursery, trying to keep her tears in check. The maids had flung open the windows to let the dreary winter air out and allow the fresh spring breeze to sweep indoors.

Bars of light poured into the house creating sharp rigid, shadows. Little specks of dust danced in the sunshine like sprites and wedding bells tolled in the distance.

Gopshall Manor felt light and cheerful for a change as if the dark, phlegmatic air had finally released its grip on the house.

She felt the north wind flee and the atmosphere warm around her, and, yet, her heart remained firmly rooted in winter.

She increased her speed as if she could outrun her tears. She forced herself to think of all that the children would need on the journey. Favourite toys, blanket, biscuits, travelling coats ....

Her skirts swished around her as she turned the corner and the breeze rushed in from the open windows, tugged at her pins, and unravelled her neat bun.

A wayward strand slipped into her eye, making her wince in pain and close her eyes, but before she could brush it away, someone gripped her arm and yanked her into an empty guest room.

"Stop fighting me," Lord Claybrook said, gripping her hands and gently pulling them away from her face. "Let me help."

She froze, and her heart began beating hard and fast.

She felt him lean towards her, and soon his face was close enough for his breath to caress her cheeks.

Her chest rose and fell in agitation, and she swallowed nervously.

Gentle hands pulled the strand away, and a warm handkerchief scented with amber and spices soothed her eye.

"Better?" he asked.

She nodded. "It doesn't sting anymore."

He stepped back, and she could breathe again.

She looked around the guest room and wrinkled her nose. Someone had forgotten to open the windows here, and the dank winter scent still clung to the periwinkle and rose curtains. Dust covered the large writing table and the windowsill, while the paisley design on the carpet had turned grey with age. Even the Paris green wallpaper had faded to a dull mossy hue in parts.

It was as if the room had forgotten to progress with the season, much like her state of mind.

"The door is shut," she said in surprise.

"I was going to tell you about the children."

She reached around him and gripped the door handle to open it.

He placed a warm, rough hand over hers to stay her. "You can leave once I have finished speaking."

"This is not seemly," she argued. "We can speak outside."

His hands shot out and gripped her waist.

She gasped as his fingers tightened, and she was lifted off the floor.

He stared up at her, holding her aloft for a moment, and then gently set her down, away from the door.

"Breathe," he commanded softly.

She obliged by gulping in a big lung full of air.

"Miss Peyton, you wouldn't want anyone else hearing what I have to say."

Something in his tone made her freeze.

He was furious, she suddenly realised, and yet his hands lingered on her small waist as if he was reluctant to release her.

His fingers dug into her skin through the thin muslin dress, and she squirmed inwardly.

She felt an incredible urge to lean into him despite the raging storm swirling in his eyes.

She tipped her head back, her eyes full of emotion. What did he want?

He cleared his throat and stepped away from her. His eyes took in the pins escaping her hair and the wrinkles in her pale-yellow morning gown where she had gripped the skirts in agitation.

She tore her gaze away from him, feeling flushed and embarrassed. They were in a bedchamber together, unchaperoned …. Her ears began to feel warm, and the sunlight streaming in through the window suddenly felt hot as fire on her skin.

He was looking at her like she was a slice of ratafia cake and he a starving orphan.

His voice when he spoke was low and husky. "I am sending the children back home where Aunt Miriam can take care of them. You must admit, being in a house with a lurking murderer is dangerous. If something happens to them –

"We can keep an eye on them here," she argued.

"Don't be ridiculous."

"You will keep them safe," she insisted.

"You have grown attached to them."

She dropped her lashes. "They have been in my care for over a year. It is natural."

"You would rather endanger them than let them go?"

He strode towards the window and flung it open, letting the sound of chirping birds and the fresh breeze fly in. The scent of spring flowers and new grass filled the room.

He stood for a moment, breathing deeply. Just when she thought he was done with the conversation, he said, "They are my children, *Miss Peyton*, I know what's best for them."

She lifted her chin defiantly. "You don't trust me."

In a single stride, he was, once again, a breath away from

her. His head dipped, and his face darkened, "I am conflicted, I admit."

She refused to be cowed. He was trying to intimidate her, and she couldn't understand why. She took a small step back to clear her head.

His eyebrow rose, his eyes dropped to her feet and back to her face.

"You think I killed Beazley?" she stuttered.

His next words were like a bucket of snow being upended on her head. "I don't want to believe it but—"

"But?"

"Unfortunately, I am forced to consider it."

She dropped her lashes, hiding her pain; pain at being separated from the children, pain at being distrusted when it was not her fault.

He reached out, gently grasped her chin and lifted it a few inches. "So many secrets."

She closed her eyes and clenched her fist. She didn't want to see his eyes, dark as the night, staring down at her, searching, asking, judging her.

Every time he looked at her in this strange, intense way, she felt darts of pain shoot through her heart.

In the ensuing silence, she felt him staring at her. The silence stretched until her every breath sounded loud and discordant.

She prayed he would speak soon, or she would lose her bearing.

She felt a puff of breath on her face, and then, as if he couldn't help it, he stroked her bottom lip with his thumb.

She gasped in shock and pleasure.

"I had written to your mother, *Miss Jane Peyton*, and received an interesting reply." His eyes hardened and sparked angrily like pieces of ice in sunlight.

Her hand flew to her neck in horror, and she swayed on her feet. "I c-can explain."

His hand shot out to grip her arm, and he slowly twisted it behind her back, making her arch against him and cry out.

Fear began coursing through her blood. He hated being lied to. He despised it.

She had seen him throw the old cook out when he discovered that he had been cheating him by selling his spices in the market.

She had seen the cook beg and plead and tell him about his sick mother and yet, he had taken him by the scruff of his neck and thrown him out.

At the same time, she had seen him call the best physician in London to tend to his loyal housekeeper when she was sick. She had seen him send sweets to all the children on his estate.

She had also seen him cruelly beat the stable hand when he found him torturing the horses.

He hated being betrayed. He could be the most generous employer, and, yet, if he found his kindness being taken advantage off, he turned into a monster; a roaring beast that frightened her.

"Do you know what your *mother* said, Miss Peyton?" His head dipped, and his lips were an inch away from her nape.

She swallowed and shook her head.

"She said I was being extremely cruel in writing to her about her beloved daughter. I was awfully insensitive in saying she worked in my house and telling her how wonderful she was as a governess. She said it was cruel since that's all her daughter had desired before her death a year ago. My letter made her sob and left rivulets of ink running down the page as she relived the moment her daughter, Miss Jane Peyton, died in her arms."

"I can explain," she repeated desperately.

"I don't know you at all," he closed his eyes briefly. "Blast it! I don't even know your name!" He shook her, and she cried out in fright.

"You are hurting me."

"No more than you have hurt me," he said, flinging her away in disgust.

"Please, let me speak."

"I can't believe a word that comes out of your mouth. What

you have done . . . nothing you say or do can redeem it," he snapped.

She gripped his hand. "I was wrong, but I never intended to keep you in the dark. I was going to confess."

"You had over a year, and in all that time you couldn't bring yourself to tell me the truth."

"I fell in love . . . with the children. I didn't want to part with them."

She shrank at the expression on his face. He was looking at her like she was a viper.

"I need to know who you are, where you are from and why you lied," he finally said. "Not because I have any desire to know more about you, but this murder has forced my hand. I am meant to investigate each member of this house, and you happen to be one of them."

He no longer appeared angry but disappointed and weary.

Her heart ached with unhappiness, and she cursed herself for deceiving him.

He opened the door and turned to face her one last time, "I will hear you out this evening in my study. Please bring all the proof you can about who you are and what your history is. I need to see letters; I need the names of people who know you and can verify your claims."

She nodded, letting tears finally flow freely down her face.

He jerked his head away from her. "I wish I could throw you out this moment, alas, this murder has forced my hand."

"Can I say goodbye to the children?"

"You will never see them again."

She ducked her head in defeat.

Chapter Thirteen

Lucy

"**F**ruit cake?"

Lucy looked up from her desk at the dishevelled little boy. "I can see the worms stuffed in the middle of it, Master Willoughby."

"I want to go for a walk."

"I am no longer your governess."

"Why?"

"Your mother thinks I killed Beazley."

"Why?"

"I do not know."

"Why?"

She narrowed her eyes at him.

He narrowed his as well. "You can still come for a walk with me."

"I have been told to stay away from you."

"Why?"

"Children shouldn't talk to people suspected of being murderers. In case I murder you, too, in a fit of rage."

"But you are so much more exciting being a murderess. Did you shoot him in the back or the front? Was there a lot of blood? I saw the corpse, it was . . . wonderful."

Lucy shuddered. The things little boys found enjoyable was singularly ghastly for most sane people. She wondered where the love for repulsive things vanished once you grew up.

She eyed Master Willoughby speculatively. She supposed it was a rite of passage; a way to glean if the creature in front of you had bounded over the childhood fence or not.

All you needed was a toad and an adolescent. If they cooed over the warty amphibian, then you had a child on your hands, but if they were repelled, then congratulations were in order since they were now sensible adults.

He stamped his foot in impatience.

She tutted irritably. "I did not kill him. Now go away. I need to finish these letters."

"But I am bored."

"You should have left with the other children."

"But they are silly babies."

"They are younger than you but far more well behaved and decidedly not silly. You are silly."

He rolled his eyes.

She ignored him, finished the letter and dusted the ink.

He stood on his toes and tried to read it.

"It's not exciting," she said. "Just a letter to my friend from the orphanage informing her that I have been accused of a heinous crime and if I am convicted, then she can have all my belongings."

He looked around the sparse room. "You don't have much."

"I am leaving. Find someone else to pester." She stood up and smoothed her skirts.

"Will you bring me something to eat from the kitchen?" he asked, following her.

"No."

"A dry biscuit. I am starving. I think I am going to die. I feel like a traveller in a desert. I was reading about that in a travelogue I found in the library. Did you know it gets very hot in the desert?"

She increased her pace, fairly flying up the stairs. She needed to start her investigation, and the first step was to eavesdrop on every member of the family. Surely someone would let something slip.

Now, who could she begin with? And how was she meant to eavesdrop without being found out?

Maybe, she could sit outside the window in the drawing-room? The rose bush underneath it was thorny, so she would have to wear thick skirts and mittens.

"Miss Trotter, are you listening?" Master Willoughby whined and yanked her sleeve.

The sleeve came off.

She froze in shock. This had never happened before. Sure, she was terrible at sewing but to have her sleeve fall off . . . She moaned.

Master Willoughby stared at the sleeve, then at her bare arm. His face split into a grin and he hugged the sleeve like it was a pirate's treasure and ran.

She gaped at the scampering boy and wondered what to do. She couldn't be seen without a sleeve . . . especially by Lady Willoughby. It would be humiliating. She had to go back to her room and change.

Just then Lady Willoughby's voice echoed down the corridor. She was heading towards her and would be upon her in moments!

She yanked open the door closest to her and flew inside.

It was the music room, she sighed in relief. No one used this room; she would be safe here.

She looked around for a place to sit. The curtains were pulled to the side, tied with gilded ropes and the light streaming in through the windows was dense with dancing dust. The sofa and the instruments were covered with big sheets of white cloth, making it startlingly bright in the room.

The footsteps came closer, and the handle began to turn.

Blast it!

She dove under the draped piano, yanked her skirt out of view just as the door opened and Lady Willoughby entered followed by the butler.

Mr Underhill, the butler, was a handsome man and had appeared most amiable until the day she had returned with Lord Adair. She knew he was keen on the milkmaid with her bright, clotted cream skin. She hoped the sweet girl would never succumb to his charms.

"At last, we are alone, my little bear," Lady Willoughby sighed.

Lucy's eyes widened in shock. She could see their feet from where she was hiding and nothing more.

"I missed you, my Butterkin," the butler responded.

The sound of kisses filled the air. A violin strummed when one of them accidentally brushed against it. The harp twanged in irritation and music sheets flew into the air and scattered close to where Lucy was hiding.

She inched closer to the edge and tried to peer upwards at the couple. Devil take it! She could see the knees but nothing higher, and if she lifted the cloth, she would be discovered.

"Oh, my pudding, my sweet, sweet aubergine pickle," Lady Willoughby said, her voice thick and soft.

Deep red, velvet gloves fluttered down to the ground, and Lucy blushed as she watched two sets of feet entwine.

The butler's jacket slid to the floor and soon his farting crackers – that is his breeches– were slithering down his thighs.

Lucy burned with curiosity. She slid a touch closer to the edge until the sheet touched the tip of her nose. She could go no further.

"Ooh," Lady Willoughby moaned. "I love chin tickles."

Lucy gagged. Chin tickles?

After a few moments of silence, where she wondered what the couple was doing, Lady Willoughby spoke again. Her voice was laboured as if she hadn't taken a breath in a long time. "Why did I have to marry that awful cowardly lump. I am glad he has moved out of our bedchamber. Perhaps, in a few days, you can join me, my little banana."

"Lord Claybrook is keeping an eye on us. We have to be careful."

"I love these secret meetings," Lady Willoughby said with a

laugh. "But I still hope my husband dies soon. Every time Lord Aston hoots at his son or leaps upon him to frighten him, I fervently pray that he gives up his ghost. My husband gives it up, I mean; though, it would be ideal if the two departed together. I wish I could do something to hasten the process."

Lucy brightened. Had she found the murderer? She cocked her head and sneezed.

It came out of nowhere. That is, the sneeze came out of nowhere. She hadn't been prepared.

Perhaps it was the dust under the piano or her lingering cold.

It had been a small sneeze. A sweet little, achoo, but instead of bringing blessings, it brought damnation.

The white sheet flew upwards, and the breech less butler peered down at her.

"I lost my sleeve, I heard footsteps and hid under here," she babbled.

Lady Willoughby grabbed her hand and dragged her out. "Lost your sleeve, did you? A likely story indeed." She tossed her towards the butler as if she was a rag doll and wiped her hands on her skirt. "I am sure she is having an affair with someone, Underhill, and her sleeve came off while she was in a passionate embrace. He must have escaped when he heard us coming. No one is this incompetent with a needle."

Lucy lifted her chin defiantly. "I am very incompetent, and I didn't mean to eavesdrop. I didn't know this room was used."

"No one will believe you," Lady Willoughby snapped.

The butler pulled on his breeches, and Lady Willoughby smoothed her hair and donned her gloves.

They began hunting for her stockings.

"No one will believe what?" Lucy asked, pointing to the green silk stockings hanging on the curtain rod. It looked like a green snake ready to strike, much like its owner.

The butler got on all fours while Lady Willoughby stood on his back. "No one will believe that you saw the two of us together, you daft looby," she said, retrieving her stockings.

Lucy shrugged. "Lord Claybrook and Lord Adair can decide

for themselves who they want to believe."

"Are you threatening us?"

"No, but if I am questioned, I have no reason to flim-flam."

"I have a lovely pearl necklace," Lady Willoughby said sweetly.

"I detest pearls."

The butler grabbed her neck, and his handsome face suddenly turned cruel and harsh. "I know how to deal with such women. Leave her to me."

The butler squeezed her neck, and she kicked and scratched to no avail.

Just when she thought she was going to die, the door flew open and Lord Aston hobbled in, aided by the valet.

Everyone froze, and their eyeballs darted hither thither to make sense of what they were seeing.

Lucy wheezed, and that set everyone into motion once again.

"Take your hands off the young woman," Lord Aston, snapped at the butler.

Mr Underhill did as he was told.

"What are you doing here?" Lady Willoughby asked suspiciously. "I thought you detested the music room, that's why it's been shut up since your wife's death."

"I was on my way to my room and heard a noise. We came to investigate. And you, my dear, what are *you* doing here."

"We too heard something and found this girl here."

Lord Aston shifted his weight and leaned on his ivory tipped walking stick. "Hardly a crime to seek some solace in an abandoned room. Were you plotting another murder?"

"We caught her stealing," the butler mumbled.

"Stealing?" Lord Aston stared around the room. "Stealing what? I doubt the woman can drag a piano out by herself or carry a harp to her room. Perhaps she fancied an old violin . . . not worth much I am afraid."

"Music sheets," Lady Willoughby said, indicating the sheets of paper strewn on the floor. "She was stealing the music sheets."

"So, you decided to murder her on the spot for a couple of

music sheets?" the valet glared at the butler.

"She was having an affair with someone. Her sleeve is missing," Lady Willoughby snapped.

"Ah, an affair. With whom?" Lord Aston asked, looking around.

"I think he fled," Lady Willoughby replied.

"I see. Well, my dear, can you tell me if you were trying to kill the girl for having an affair with an unknown person, or was it for the music sheets. It's all a bit muddled, I am afraid."

"I have to go," Lucy choked out. "I didn't try to steal anything, nor was I having an affair." She didn't dare to mention what she had seen. After all, the butler had almost throttled her to death and if she confessed . . . She shuddered and touched her sore neck.

She raced out of the room, her heart thundering, and her ears ringing. No one stopped her.

She took big gulps of air as she ran, feeling glad that she was alive.

It was entirely possible that the butler and Lady Willoughby had plotted to kill her husband. It was also clear they were lovers and had been for a long time.

And Lord Aston and the valet . . . What had they been doing outside the music room?

Lord Aston rarely ventured anywhere on his feet. He was always carried in his chair.

He preferred to stay in his room, or the dining room where all the fireplaces were kept roaring for him to be able to sit in his unmentionables. The only other place he enjoyed going to was the oriental garden when it was a clear day, and the sun was high and sharp in the sky.

She collapsed on her bed and stared at the peeling roof. Something was bothering her. Something Lord Aston had said . . . she frowned and tried to replay the event as it happened.

Her eyes widened as it came to her. He had said he had been going to his room when he heard a noise. An entirely logical explanation, except for the fact that his room was in a completely

different wing of the house.
  He had lied, but why?

Chapter Fourteen

Jane

The sun was about to set, and the dense clouds muted the evening light to a pale orange and gold.

It was a warm evening with thousands of water droplets suspended in the air. Jane mopped her face with a handkerchief as she slowly made her way towards the study.

She hoped the bundle of letters she had gathered was enough to prove her identity.

He would finally know her truth, and, yet, he would never forgive her for her deceit. Her heart felt leaden, and her stomach churned in anxiety. This was not how she had wanted him to find out.

This wasn't how it was all supposed to end.

She paused outside the study door, and her courage failed spectacularly. She couldn't face him. She felt awful. This whole situation was awful.

She had eaten nothing since he had told her he knew about her lie. The dark, tepid tea she had drunk just before coming to see him was making her feel worse. Mayhap the cook had thrown in a dash of spoilt milk.

Gopshall Manor rose around her like an unfriendly, oppressive creature. She hated this house. She hated how isolated she was here, like a forgotten, barren island constantly assailed by furious, angry waves.

The servants, who had previously been warm to her, had formed a unit. They believed that it was the two outsiders who had killed Beazley. It couldn't be one of their own.

It was no different from how the family felt, she supposed, but it was still disheartening to see such a drastic change in their behaviour. Only two days ago, she had been chatting with the cook about her life in the country, and today the woman wouldn't even meet her eye.

"Come in, Miss Peyton," Lord Claybrook called out.

She hadn't knocked nor made a sound, and, yet, he had sensed her presence.

"Come in," he repeated impatiently.

She took a deep breath and opened the door.

The two fireplaces in the room were cold, and no one had thought to light them again. She wondered if she should do it. Lord Claybrook must be chilled to the bone working in such a room for hours.

The expression on his face warned her to stay put. She pulled the shawl tighter around herself, trying not to shiver. Her cheap slippers were not adequate for the icy stone floor, and she curled her toes in a feeble attempt to warm them.

"Sit."

"I would rather stand."

"I said sit down."

"No."

"Do you want me to force you into the chair?"

She decided to save her breath and slid into the seat.

He looked tired and angry. Disappointment and loathing shone in his eyes whenever he happened to glance her way.

It cut her like a knife, and she sat up straighter. "Here are the letters explaining everything."

"Leave them on the desk. I will read them later to verify the truth of your statement. But they are not going to be enough."

"This is all I have," she responded, her voice defiant.

"Watch your tongue," he said sharply. "It seems you no longer need to act the sweet, calm governess. Your claws are coming out."

"You won't believe anything I say, so why even bother discussing this?"

"You have deceived me, lied to me. Don't you think you owe me an explanation?"

"I do." She dropped her lashes, feeling ashamed. She didn't know why she was so defensive. He was right, she had no right to speak to him like this.

He stood up and came around the desk. He leaned his hip against the table and stared down at her.

Her heart thundered, and she shrank in her seat. Her fingers dug into her skirts, and her eyes dropped to the floor. The scent of exotic wood and cigars enveloped her.

He picked up a snuffbox lying on the table and tossed it from hand to hand while he waited for her to speak.

She glanced at the snuffbox, sparkling in the light, and then carefully focussed on the window as she pondered what to say.

The window was slightly open, she realised, and the rain scented breeze trickled in, keeping the temperature down. The rose garden and the sky outside appeared dreary, and the trees swayed in the distance as if battling a storm. It seemed as if someone had leached all colour from the world and left behind shades of grey.

Now that she thought of it, Lord Claybrook always kept the rooms a touch chilly. She frowned. Was it because his father, Lord Aston, always kept the rooms uncomfortably hot? Perhaps this contrary behaviour hinted at a troubled relationship between them.

He cleared his throat, prompting her to begin.

"My name is Elizabeth Verney," she said, her voice trembling a touch. "I am the youngest of seven sisters, and I had needed employment urgently. My family is poor, and they couldn't afford to keep me much longer. My bosom friend, Lady Jane Peyton, lived in our village, and she was in a similar situation. She needed work just as much as I did. We applied for a few posts together, and Jane got your offer within a month. But the letter came too late. She was on her death bed, dying of pneumonia."

"You used your friend's death to your advantage," he said disgustedly. "You decided to impersonate her?"

She closed her eyes; his hard voice was like a dagger slashing at her most vulnerable spot. "I used to visit her," she continued quietly. "I used to read to her, books, letters and women's magazines. One day, I happen to come across your letter, the one where you offered her the post of a governess."

She swallowed and continued. "She knew I wasn't a lady; hence, finding such a good home would have been impossible for me. So, she asked me to take the job. She said no one would know, and I could earn some money and help my poor mother. Meanwhile, I could continue looking for a post under my real name."

"You have been looking for another post?"

She nodded. "I haven't had much luck, but it's only a matter of time before someone agrees to hire me."

"You wanted to leave us?" he gripped her arm and yanked her up. "You got us all used to your ways, and then one day you would have just left?"

"I-I didn't think it was right to continue under a false name."

"You could have told me the truth."

"I don't think you would have hired me if you had known the truth."

"How could you deceive us, Miss Verney?"

"I didn't want to." A tear trickled down her nose and fell on his arm.

He stared down at her face, looking torn. "I don't know what to believe. I don't know what to think. What you did was horrible . . . and, yet, I don't believe you killed Beazley. You lied to me, yes, but I cannot see you as a ruthless killer." He pushed her away, making her stumble. "But what do I know? You fooled me for over a year . . . for all I know you are a cold-blooded criminal."

"I am not," she cried. "I lied, and I am sorry. I was desperate, but I would never hurt anyone."

"You have hurt *us*," he snapped. "You have hurt the children. They will miss you."

"Do you believe me?"

"I have asked Lord Adair to investigate your background. Until I get word from him, I will believe nothing out of your mouth. I pray this time you have spoken the truth."

"I wish I could leave," she said, turning away.

"I wish you could, too."

Chapter Fifteen

Lucy

Lucy's woollen skirts and thick mittens protected her from the thorny rose bush, but her legs were beginning to ache from crouching under the study window for so long. When a raindrop fell on her nose, she decided that she had heard enough and crawled away.

She hopped up and Spinoza swooped down and landed on her hat. She tightened the scarf around her ears and began walking towards the apple orchard.

"I should return indoors, Spinoza, but after all that I have found out . . . I simply have to walk and think."

Lady Jane Peyton was Miss Elizabeth Verney? It couldn't be!

Spinoza squawked in protest as it began drizzling.

"I cannot believe it. She seemed so innocent, well-mannered and so, so . . . good. If anything, I felt completely inadequate in front of her. She seemed so sensible."

The raindrops became fatter, and she hurriedly took shelter under a giant statue of Venus, holding a pot of flowers. The pot was large enough to shield her hat and Spinoza from the worst of it.

"Lady Jane Peyton has turned out to be an ordinary Miss Elizabeth Verney." She suddenly laughed as she extended her arms and let the droplets dance on her fingertips. "Oh, how brilliant. That girl is an excellent actress. As for her actions, who am

I to judge?"

In fact, she completely sympathised with Elizabeth. She had seen poverty and misery while at the orphanage, seen the desperation in the eyes of those in pangs of hunger, and witnessed death shatter bonds between friends. She, too, would have asked her friend to take her place had she been in Jane's position.

No, she didn't blame the girl, just admired her for pulling the whole thing off for so long.

She also pitied Jane, or rather, Elizabeth, to call her by her real name. She had lost her chance at romancing and marrying Lord Claybrook. She was not an impoverished lady, and an affair between them would be nothing short of scandalous.

Elizabeth was a wonderful governess who adored children. Even Master Willoughby listened to her and did her bidding. Perhaps, Lord Adair would be able to find another post for her?

Master Willoughby. She scowled. That boy still had her sleeve. He was going to be the death of her.

Spinoza squawked again, but this time he sounded anxious.

Her neck prickled; someone was watching her. She surveyed the landscape, cursing her poor eyesight.

The blurred shadows in the distance made her shiver nervously. Perhaps, it was better not to venture out alone anymore. Not after the way the butler had threatened to kill her. She turned back towards the house, her heart racing.

The feeling that someone was watching her stayed with her until she reached her room. She closed the door and put a chair against it and sat at her desk.

Spinoza flew to the top of the cupboard and tucked his head under his wing.

She pulled out a parchment and dipped the quill in ink, her hands cold and the quill shaky.

She felt as if fear had crept into Gopshall Manor and made itself at home. The fact that a murderer lurked in their midst had seeped into its walls and furnishings, making the manor seem dense, dark and sinister.

It was a cold sort of fear, that left everyone anxious, watchful and suspicious. Time seemed to have stretched unbearably, and she felt as if any moment, she would break with a twang.

A drop of ink fell from the nib onto the parchment. She watched it spread, a frown on her pale, fragile face. Mayhap, things would become clearer if she wrote them down. And the task would take her mind off the lingering dread and fear lurking in her stomach.

Lady Catherine Willoughby.

She stared at the name thoughtfully for a moment before continuing:

Alibi: She says she was with her lady's maid, Rosie.

Motive: She detests her husband and wants to kill him to be free to carry on an affair with the butler?

What if her target had been Beazley? He could have been a past lover and had been blackmailing her? Or he had seen her canoodling with the butler and threatened to reveal her secret?

She chewed the quill and realised it was the inky nib in her mouth. She spluttered and spat for a moment, before writing down the next name.

Mr Underhill, the butler.

Mediocre at his job but a charming young man with a well-hidden cruel streak.

Alibi: Do not know

Motive: Is having an affair with Lady Willoughby and wants Lord Willoughby out of the way.

Beazley caught them together, and he had to kill him.

A shiver ran down her spine as she once again recalled his large hand, squeezing her neck.

The butler could have done it.

She swallowed and took a deep breath to reassure herself that she was safe.

"By Jove, Spinoza, what with having my neck squeezed and witnessing farting crackers sliding down the butler's thighs, I am beginning to creak, and it won't be long before I detach from the hinges," she sighed. "I need a nob by my side, old bird. I need Lord Adair."

Chapter Sixteen

Elizabeth

Elizabeth heard Lord Claybrook talking to the valet outside the drawing-room. She couldn't face him, not after he had discovered her truth.

She could feel her neck turning red and ears getting warm. She had to hide.

She looked around desperately. The curtains . . . no, he preferred standing by the window, she would be caught in a moment.

The room was filled with all sorts of useless things like porcelain cats, ivory statues and golden footstools. The curio cupboard was brimming with knick-knacks, from teacups to fossils but had no place for a human to hide.

The fainting couch? Oh, the devil take it! It was too narrow for her to fit under.

He was at the door! Her fingers flew to her mouth in fright. She could hear his voice ringing clear as day.

It would have to be the giant blue and silver vase in the corner. It was a beautiful piece, hand-painted and filled with a bunch of dried lavender flowers. It came up to her shoulder, and she hoped it was wide enough for her to squeeze into.

She leapt towards it, yanked the dried flowers out, and using a footstool, slid into the belly of the vessel. It was a tight fit, and she had to almost curl into herself to stay hidden from the view.

She gathered the dried flowers and held them aloft, and hoped they appeared no different from outside.

The deuced man had an eagle eye and an elephant's memory. If a leaf were out of place, he would probably notice.

She held her breath as she heard footsteps enter the room.

Lord Claybrook was moving around the room, she realised. What was he doing? She could hear a lot of rustling, and was that a clink of china? Surely, that sounded like someone patting the cushions.

She frowned in confusion and wished she could hop up and see what was going on.

And then the oddest thing happened, he came up to where she was hiding and pushed aside a few dried flowers.

She watched in terror as two male fingers tossed a piece of paper into the vase and hurriedly fluffed up the flowers again.

The paper landed on her lap, and she clutched it in fright.

The footsteps receded, and she heard the door close. She heaved a sigh of relief and sprang up.

The door flew open just then, and Claybrook walked in.

Her mouth fell open, and she gasped in horror.

He eyed her back in shock and confusion.

Her eyelids began twitching nervously, as the reality of the position she was in, crashed upon her. She was standing in a vase, clutching a handful of dried flowers. She closed her eyes and hoped this was all a bad dream.

"What on earth are you doing?"

She gulped. "I am not sure how to explain—"

"Spying?"

She shook her head. "No, I was . . . changing these flowers. They have become dusty."

"I see, and you felt the need to climb into the vase rather than pull them out like most people would have done because?"

"I wanted to be thorough. What if some flowers fell into the bottom of the vase?"

"You do know that you are talking utter nonsense, *Miss Verney?*"

She ducked her head. "I know."

"That thing must be full of spiders. I thought women detested such—"

With a squeal, Elizabeth threw the flowers into the air and tried to clamber out. The vase began to tip—He was beside her in a trice, holding the vase steady with one hand while lifting her out with the other.

Her eyes squeezed shut, and she clutched his shirt as the thought of spiders racing through her clothes filled her with dread.

Her racing heart steadied finally, and she realised she was still in his arms. With a squeak, she detached herself from him and took a few steps back. "I am sorry."

His expression was thunderous. She was reminded of a furious, caged lion waiting for the gate to open so he could pounce and demolish his prey.

She took another step back and almost fell over the fire poker. His hand shot out, but she steadied herself before he could touch her.

She watched as his fingers curled into a fist and dropped to his side.

"Deuced woman," he muttered, irritably, and turned on his heels and strode out.

She watched him leave, and it was only after she was back in her room, dusting herself off and looking for spiders in her bodice did she remember the letter.

She pulled it out and read it.

Deer Mr Undyhil

I ave asket a frand to rite this. My ma says that if mr undyhil wants to go undy my skurt then ee must marry me. I do feel we soot eech other so yes, I weel marry you.

yours

Lamby, the milkmaid

Her eyebrow rose. The man who had hidden the letter had been the butler. She folded the letter and tucked it into her reticule.

So, the two of them were in love, how sweet. It was nice to come upon a bit of happiness at such times. She would return the letter as soon as she saw him; until then, she would keep it safe.

∞∞∞

Lucy

Lucy's hand trembled as she carefully replaced the vase on the pedestal. Her stomach was clenched and sweat beaded her brow. She could not believe that she had decided to follow Mr Underhill, the butler. The man who had tried to squeeze the life out of her and frightened her so much that she had spent the entire night awake like a hungry owl.

In the dark, with nothing but a spluttering candle to keep her company, every sound had been magnified, every rustle had made her start, and every shadow had appeared threatening. The ghost of Aunt Sedley had not terrified her as much as this blasted man had. And yet, she had decided to follow him today to find out as much as she could about him.

She was an utter loon.

She blinked rapidly to banish her dread. It was daylight, and she was safe. She took a deep breath, opened the back door and scurried after the butler.

Until now, he had done nothing unremarkable except lurk outdoors in the misty morning light, like a shifty fox.

He had perked up briefly at the sight of the scullery maid who had been away for the last few days tending her sick mother. He had filled her in, rather eagerly, about the murder.

The young girl had listened wide-eyed and open-mouthed. She had been horribly fascinated and thanked her stars for being away from it all, for had she seen the dead man, she declared dramatically, she would have died of fright.

The butler moved on from the scullery maid to the carriage driver and once again regaled the news to the driver, enjoying every flicker of horrified emotion on the man's face.

"I have some of the dead man's toenail clippings," the butler muttered under his breath. "I am willing to sell them. I might even have his shirt. The one he was wearing the day he was murdered. It has bloodstains."

Lucy, peering at him from behind a large prickly bush, scowled in disgust. She knew it was a fashion for people to purchase a murder victim's belongings, and if the victim happened to be a nob, then the price was even higher. But to have the butler of the house make such underhand dealings . . . she tsked quietly.

Mr Underhill was a terrible butler. He was a gossip and a fop who was more concerned about the state of his jacket than his duties. Rather than protect the secrets of his master, he was scattering them about like birdseed.

She tapped her foot impatiently.

Other than displaying his havy cavy ways, he had done nothing else of interest. He had not even attempted to venture towards Lady Willoughby's room where Lucy had hoped he might give away some information in throes of passion.

When he ventured indoors, she almost gave up the chase, since following him inside the house was not an easy task. Any moment now, someone could call her name and she would be caught.

She clutched the cheap earring in her hand; an excuse in case someone found her lurking under tables or skulking behind pillars and she could say she was looking for it. But she doubted the butler would fall for the ruse.

She watched him enter the kitchen and paused, wondering what to do next. Give up the chase? She hadn't been welcomed in the kitchen since the murder, so she had steered clear of the place, only popping in to get a tray to eat in her room.

Then she recalled the noose dangling over her head and squared her shoulders. That was far more frightening than dealing with a bunch of grumpy servants. She would make her own pot of tea, just the way she liked it, and the cook could simmer and whistle in the corner for all she cared.

The kitchen was toasty since the flames flickering in the large fireplace had warmed up the wooden floors.

The cook sat at the worn wooden table peeling a giant bowl of potatoes. Rosie and Mary, the maids, sat with their heads together at the far end of the table. The scullery maid, looking gaunt and tired lingered by the fire, standing as close to it as she dared.

"A cup of tea?" the butler requested from his position by the door. He sat in an old rocking chair, his legs spread out, eyes closed, and his fingers steepled on his stomach.

The cook poured him a cup, and Lucy's eyebrow shot upwards when she saw her put a spoon of sugar into it. She had done it so swiftly that no one else noticed.

Sugar was carefully rationed in this house along with everything else. Lord Aston did not think the servants should be allowed such luxuries. Neither did he believe the cook needed a kitchen maid or Lady Willoughby, a housekeeper.

No one dared to go against the old man's wishes since he had complete control of Gopshall finances.

She eyed the jars of preserved pineapples, exotic spices and chocolates sitting high up on the shelf in the kitchen cupboard, as well as the big lumps of meat hanging on ropes in the larder.

Almost everyone was deprived of luxuries, she corrected herself. Lord Willoughby could spend as he saw fit; after all, he was the heir to Gopshall Manor and enjoyed diving at foodstuff.

She watched as the cook handed over the teacup and the butler took a sip and closed his eyes. If the cook had expected some sort of acknowledgement for the risk she had taken, then she was disappointed.

Was the cook in love with the butler? Sure, he was a handsome man, but the cook was old enough to be his mother. The round, red-faced portly woman with a head full of grey curls didn't seem the type to go chasing after pretty boys.

She watched the old woman as she stood for a moment staring down at the butler. The woman had a look of loathing on her face that startled her: not love but hate. The cook hated the butler.

The cook turned just then and spotted Lucy lurking at the entrance.

"Your tray is by the stove," the cook said, all evidence of previous emotion vanishing from her face. She sat back on the table and continued peeling potatoes as if nothing had happened.

Lucy took the tray, but instead of leaving, she placed it on the kitchen table, opposite the cook. She pulled the chair back, and the sound it made as it slid across the wooden floor had every pair of eyes swivel towards her.

She ignored them, sat down, and calmly began to eat.

The cook opened and closed her mouth a few times as if searching for words. Unable to find any, she turned towards the maids and began discussing her neighbours. Her favourite and safe topic.

"I went home last night," the cook told the girls. "Ran into Mrs Lay's eldest daughter. She distinctly smelled of gin."

"Nay, truly?" Rosie asked, fascinated.

"And who do you think came right behind her?"

"Not Mr Timber?" Rosie screeched.

"Oh yes, it was Mr Timber, alright. I saw him with my own eyes, not ten paces away from the girl."

Lucy had loved listening to the escapades of the cook's immoral neighbours. She had missed this.

She shoved a spoon full of peas into her mouth and leaned forward to hear more. At the same time, she happened to glance towards the butler and froze. He was glaring at her. The threat and warning in his eyes sparkled like the embers in the fire.

The food turned to dust in her mouth, and she lost interest in the cook's silly gossip. She picked up the tray and left the room.

Chapter Seventeen

Elizabeth

"Who is it?"

"It's me."

Elizabeth put her spoon down and opened the door.

Lucy stood with a tray laden with her dinner, her expression hesitant. "Can we eat together. I hate eating alone and what with the servants treating us both like chamber pots, I thought we could give each other company."

Elizabeth smiled. She had been tired of eating her meals in the dark, windowless room. It had become depressing. She was glad Lucy had decided to join her. "Come in."

Lucy smiled back and bounded into the room.

The dinner was plain. A few bits of meat in a watery stew, hard bread, cheese and mashed peas. For pudding, they had been given a bowl of cold stewed apple.

Elizabeth forced herself to chew a bit of the bread. She glanced at her companion and found Lucy eating her dinner as if it were a gourmet meal. She supposed living in the orphanage had taught her to appreciate every morsel.

They ate silently, each comfortable in the other's presence. This soothing companionship was new.

They had been acquaintances living in the same house, and their specific duties had kept them too busy to idle away time in gossiping and making friends.

Besides, their very nature was so different that Elizabeth didn't think they could ever be friends and yet, watching Lucy sitting by her side eating animatedly, she couldn't help but feel a touch of fondness for her.

Lucy Anne Trotter, she pondered the name and the girl. Such a simple name and yet, the girl was unique.

The entire household treated her like an unwanted fruit fly. Even the servants mocked her, for they, at least, knew where they came from.

And yet, Lucy wore her happy face like a shield. The cold glances and the sneers seemed to bounce off her skin.

She was loony, true, but she was also wonderfully brave. After all, she had stolen a horse and ridden all the way to Lord Adair's house at the tail end of a snowstorm.

Someone else in her place would have given up and succumbed to those more powerful than her.

She was like a beautiful honeysuckle, that clambered over the ugly bits in life and covered them with dense, fragrant flowers. She was also stubborn, touched in the head and impulsive, but these quirks added to her charm.

She smiled at Lucy, thinking what a wonderfully lovable creature she was, just like a little sister.

"*A bird never flew with one wing*. We need to investigate together," Lucy said, scooping up the last apple morsel.

Elizabeth pushed her own uneaten stew towards Lucy and nodded. "I would love to help you, but I don't know how to investigate."

"Two minds are better than one. And I need help. I cannot do this alone," Lucy said. "But first we have to trust each other. I need to know everything you know, and I will tell you all that I have found out. No secrets."

Elizabeth froze. No secrets. Did Lucy know that she wasn't Jane? No, it was impossible. The conversation between her and Claybrook had been private. And since the rest of the family hadn't commented on it, she knew Claybrook had yet to share the news with everyone.

"Do you trust me?" Lucy asked.

Elizabeth nodded slowly. She trusted Lucy but not enough. The girl was a survivor. If she became desperate, she could use her deception as a way of shifting blame and escaping herself.

Lucy waited a little longer and then with a sigh, which almost sounded like disappointment, continued, "Well, I trust you. I know you didn't kill Beazley and I know I didn't kill him. That is all I am certain of. I am desperate to find the killer and get away from this place."

"How can I help?" Elizabeth straightened her spine and leaned forward. She was just as desperate to leave the manor as Lucy. She couldn't bear the sight of Claybrook anymore. Couldn't bear to see the disgust and suspicion in his eyes whenever he looked at her.

She had to get away from it all. His every glance seemed to be chipping away a part of her, and soon she would be reduced to a pile of sawdust.

The only way she could end her torment was by finding the culprit and leaving as soon as possible.

She had received a letter in the post that morning that had sounded promising. An offer to take care of an elderly woman in her home. To be her companion and a nurse.

She had wanted to be a governess, but this post was the only thing she had been offered in months. She could no longer choose to be picky, and she intended to write back as soon as possible and accept it.

The pay was low, but hopefully, with her food and board paid for, it would be enough. Time would tell.

"If you have nothing to tell me," Lucy paused, and when Elizabeth shook her head, she continued, "I have a lot to share."

Elizabeth listened open-mouthed to all Lucy had to say. The encounter with the butler shocked her, and she gasped in horror.

Lady Willoughby and the butler were having an affair? And poor Lucy, to have almost been killed when she discovered it.

She shook her head in amazement.

"Why would the butler kill Beazley?" she asked. "True he tried to strangle you, but that does not necessarily mean he killed Beazley. Why would he?"

Lucy leaned forward, her eyes bright and sparkling. "Remember, the bullet was meant for Lord Willoughby. If the butler is having an affair with Lady Willoughby, then he is the most likely suspect. He would be desperate to get rid of Lord Willoughby. Even Lady Willoughby is miserable being married to him. She looks at him with such loathing that it makes me shiver. He could have fired the shot, or Lady Willoughby did it. Either way, they are in this together."

"Lawks! I never thought of that."

"So, the butler has a motive," Lucy continued. "Now we need to know where he was at the time of the murder and the only person who has that information is Lord Claybrook."

Elizabeth's eyes widened at the look Lucy was giving her. "I am not asking Lord Claybrook." She couldn't even enter the room he was in these days, let alone seek him out and question him.

Oddly, Lucy didn't argue the point. Instead, she said, "You don't have to speak to him. When he interviewed me, I noticed he was making notes. He must have done the same for everyone he questioned. I think if we search the study, we are bound to come upon them. They will contain everyone's alibi and prove invaluable to our investigation."

Elizabeth relaxed slightly. "So all we have to do is sneak into the study and go through his papers."

"Precisely. And with two of us hunting, the job will be done quicker."

"Oh, I almost forgot." She went and got the love letter the butler had tossed into the vase and showed it to Lucy.

Lucy quickly scanned it and scowled. "The poor thing. We must save her from the blackguard."

"I agree." Elizabeth put her hand out and firmly shook Lucy's hand. "Partners in crime?" she asked with a nervous laugh.

"Partners in crime," Lucy grinned. "Here's to our first big adventure."

The two swallowed their pale, cold tea, and at that moment, it tasted as good as champagne.

Chapter Eighteen

Lucy

"Lady Willoughby is having a dinner party tonight," Lucy whispered.

"Why do we have to climb a tree to discuss this?" Elizabeth grumbled.

"I am afraid of heights, and I am trying to rid myself of it."

"By sitting atop a tree?"

"I am trembling like a wet kitten; I might freeze on the way down and fall and break my neck, but I have to learn to face my fears and get over them."

"You are a loon."

"Thank you. I also have another reason for choosing this spot. So, we are not overheard. Walls have ears."

"They do not."

"Fine. People have ears, and everyone seems to be lurking and eavesdropping these days."

"True, I saw Lord Aston urging the valet to crawl on all fours towards the drawing-room."

"He probably wanted the valet to jump out at Lord Willoughby and frighten him again. The last time he did it, Lord Willoughby had leapt out of his inexpressibles in fright."

Lucy leaned back against the branch and looked up at the bright blue sky. The broad branch was comfortable, and she momentarily forgot that she was high above the ground and a single wrong move could send her hurtling towards death.

She gazed at the luminous clouds as they moved across the sky in a gentle, lethargic manner. They appeared to be lit from within, as if a tiny creature sat in the middle of each misty puff holding a lamp.

She smiled, wishing the moment would pause forever. "I saw a few daffodils today."

Elizabeth plucked a leaf from a branch above her head and sniffed it. "I spotted a yellow daisy."

A pleasant breeze blew across the sunlit field and ruffled the girls' hair.

"I am surprised Lady Willoughby is having a dinner party. Shouldn't the family be in mourning?" Elizabeth mused.

"He wasn't family."

"But he died here. It seems a bit morbid to celebrate so soon."

Lucy produced a mushy fruit cake from her pocket and began picking out the raisins and flicking them away. She detested raisins. "Lady Willoughby has no choice. People have been curious about the murder. The newspapers have been full of it, and with no clear explanation forthcoming, the family's reputation is at stake."

"But how is Lady Willoughby throwing dinner parties rather than mourning until the culprit is found, going to help the family? It will make things worse."

Lucy watched a squirrel bound across the lawn. "I overheard Rosie tell the cook that the family have decided to invite some influential people who can urge the newspapers to show the family in a more favourable light. They will explain the circumstance as much as they can. They cannot keep hiding the facts forever. It makes them seem suspect."

Elizabeth nodded in understanding. "People are starting to get angry. I overheard Lady Willoughby telling Rosie that Lord Beazley's mother wants the entire family guillotined."

"By George! no wonder Lord Aston hurriedly agreed to the dinner."

"So," Elizabeth went on, "they have invited some powerful

people to dampen the situation until the culprit is found. They are just as frightened of the noose as we are."

"That about sums it up. I think this is an excellent time for us to search the study. It would be easier and quicker to search in a warmly lit room, rather than stumbling around in the dark with a candle. I speak from experience."

"What if someone decides to venture out during dinner?"

"No one would dare."

"These people sound far more important than the likes of the Willoughby's," Elizabeth protested. "And powerful people are often odd. Lady Willoughby told me about a guest of hers who used to travel with a Bengal tiger. He used to sit right at the dinner table—the tiger that is—along with the other guests wearing a bib and eating a lump of raw meat. Such people don't care about propriety."

"Maybe that odd guest will come today and provide us with a diversion," Lucy said hopefully.

"Not likely. The man moved to India and hasn't been heard from since. It is speculated that the tiger ate him on the long journey."

"Oh."

"We really must ensure that no one catches us, Lucy, or we will be in trouble. They will be convinced we killed Beazley together if they find us snooping in the study."

Lucy closed her eyes and tilted her face up to the sun. It had been so long since the sun had shone so brightly and warmly. She wanted to forget about her troubles and bask in the heat for a while.

A small cough behind her made her sit up with a gasp.

"Master Willoughby?" Elizabeth asked horrified.

Behind the thick tree trunk on which Lucy had just been leaning so pleasurably, appeared a mop of golden hair. Small blue eyes peered at them, and sun-warmed cheeks formed two round blobs as he smiled.

"I didn't mean to listen," he said quickly. "But I heard it all."

The girls exchanged a frightened look.

"I like you," he said, staring at Lucy. "My sister and I always did. You are different. You make us laugh."

"You tortured me."

He smiled even more broadly. "We couldn't help it. You bring it out in us."

"Well, what are you going to do about what you overheard?" Elizabeth cut in.

"Why help you," he batted his lashes, "naturally."

"I don't trust you," Lucy scowled.

"On my honour," he said, placing his hand on his heart. "It's awfully dull, having no one to talk to, and helping you will give me something to do."

"Don't believe him," Lucy whispered to Elizabeth. "He is going to go running to his mother at any moment."

"I believe him," Elizabeth whispered back. "Besides, what do we have to lose? He can tell them, and we will be doomed, but if he is honest, then we have everything to gain."

Lucy eyed the boy speculatively. She supposed Elizabeth was right. As for trusting Master Willoughby . . . he was not all that abominable. After all, he was extraordinarily gentle with his little sister and did his best to keep her happy. His mischief was harmless, with an intent to vex rather than hurt. Perhaps, deep under the layers of grime, he had a good heart.

She finally thawed and asked, "What will you do?"

He whooped in delight. "Thank you, Miss Trotter, for putting your faith in me. I shall not fail you. It is the matter of my family name. I shall succeed in my task and pray you find the answers you seek."

"You have been reading," Lucy said in amazement.

"Nothing else to do," he shrugged.

Lucy felt a pang of pity for the boy. She leaned over and patted his head.

He jerked out of her grasp. "I am not a child."

"Do you have a plan?" Elizabeth asked.

"I am going to make one. Should be easy enough."

"How will you distract them?"

"I can insist on reciting the longest poem I know?" he suggested.

"Fine, at sharp eight, we will meet you outside the dining room. Hopefully, everyone will be seated by then," Lucy said.

"This all sounds very vague. A lot can go wrong," Elizabeth muttered. "What if the poem is not long enough?"

"Courage," Lucy clapped her hands together. "Master Willoughby will not let us down."

He turned pink at the compliment and puffed out his chest. "I shall not let you down," he echoed confidently.

Chapter Nineteen

Lucy

The dinner party was in full swing. Lucy, Elizabeth and Master Willoughby watched the guests arrive from the nursery window. Carriages rolled up to Gopshall Manor, and finely dressed people clambered out, eager to learn the facts of the murder.

Some hurried in, heads bent, eyes pinned to the ground. Some alighted from the carriage, took a moment to cast a judgmental eye on the manor before strolling indoors, while the rest tip-toed in; hats pulled low, eyes darting hither-thither like badly disguised detectives.

"That young lady forgot her breeches," Master Willoughby observed.

Lucy smacked his head. "She is wearing a dress, the skirt of which is a touch sheer."

"A touch?" Elizabeth muttered under her breath. "From where I am standing, the boy is right."

"Another carriage," Lucy cried. "Oh, look, that poor young lady was caught in the rain. I hope someone gives her a new gown quickly."

"It didn't rain today," Master Willoughby observed.

Elizabeth grinned. "It's the latest fashion."

"What?" Lucy's eyebrows rose in horror. "To arrive dripping like a river rat to a dinner party is fashionable?"

"She will ruin the cushions," Elizabeth mused.

"She will catch a cold and die," Master Willoughby commented thoughtfully.

Just then, the wind changed, from north to east, and a sense of danger engulfed the girls.

The door flew open, and Lady Willoughby walked in wearing a gorgeous green and pink silk gown. Her golden ringlets shone in the light of the setting sun, and her eyes sparkled like an icy green pond.

Lady Willoughby glanced at Elizabeth's hand, resting on Master Willoughby's shoulder and scowled.

Elizabeth bit her lip and backed away.

"Johnny," Lady Willoughby hugged her stepson. "I told you to stay away from them." She dropped her voice, "They are witches in disguise."

Master Willoughby rolled his eyes and winked at Lucy.

Lucy grinned and stuck her tongue out at Lady Willoughby's back.

"Get out, Miss Trotter," Lady Willoughby said quietly. "And take your friend with you."

The odd tone in her voice sent a chill down Lucy's spine. She grasped Elizabeth's hand and quickly left the room.

"She hates us," Elizabeth muttered as they walked down the corridor towards the hidden servant's staircase.

Lucy swallowed nervously. "She can't even bear to look at you or say your name these days. I thought she disliked me far more."

Elizabeth closed her eyes briefly and straightened her shoulders. "Forget her and let's focus on our next task."

Lucy gave a sharp nod. "I am ready."

The grandfather clock in the hallway began to chime, and the girls sprinted down the stairs, tiptoed down the hall and came to a stop outside the study, before it had finished ringing the eighth bell.

The merry music of the orchestra beating through the house further muffled the sounds of their actions.

Lucy stuck her ear to the door while Elizabeth tried to peer under the doorway for any sign of human life.

The sound of someone banging away at the piano made it hard for them to hear properly. Lucy glanced at Elizabeth and raised her brow.

Elizabeth took a deep breath and gave a firm nod.

Lucy smiled, turned the handle and snuck inside. Elizabeth hurried in after her.

No one was in the room. The girls let out a sigh of relief in unison.

Lucy's heart was beating fast, and she was surprised to find Elizabeth flushed with excitement as well. She had never thought the staid girl had it in her to find anything dangerous remotely fun.

The flames in the fireplace were soft, low and spitting and hissing as if hungry for more wood. They cast a warm light and threw flickering shadows around the room.

The bookshelf, the big mahogany desk in the middle of the room, the sofa and the ornate brocade chairs were partially lit and seemed all sharp angles in the dim light.

"I feel like someone is lurking in the shadows," Elizabeth said. "Any moment a creature will leap out from behind the curtain and—"

"And?"

"Eat us," she shivered.

Lucy strode over to the curtains and flung them back to reveal the frosted windowpanes. She crouched to check behind the desk and a moment later, popped up with a smile. "We are alone."

"You are brave," Elizabeth said, admiringly.

Lucy shrugged. "If you delay an unpleasant task, then fear catches up with you and pockets your courage. You just have to move faster than fear."

"Move faster than fear. You say the oddest things," Elizabeth said, looking amused. "We better get to it then. You take this end of the desk, and I will begin looking here."

Lucy glanced at the burning candle in the middle of the table and frowned. She didn't want to alarm Elizabeth, but no one in the house would waste a beeswax candle, knowing how Lord Aston felt about money.

It was possible that someone had stepped out for a few moments and had every intention of coming back. But everyone was having dinner . . . Surely no family member would dare to refuse to attend such an important party.

A beeswax candle also ruled out the servants.

"Hurry," Elizabeth hissed.

Lucy silently cursed herself. She had just been advising Elizabeth about overthinking things, and here she was, doing just that. She approached the desk and began inspecting the papers. Her eyes and fingers flew over the papers, perhaps, less efficiently than she would have liked.

Elizabeth seemed equally panicked. Her eyes seemed to fly over the words even more speedily than Lucy's.

"Shh," Lucy whispered. "I think . . . goodness me, footsteps!"

The girls dove under the desk, ears quivering in fear.

The footsteps passed by, and they breathed a sigh of relief.

"Must be a servant," Elizabeth whispered.

Lucy didn't reply. Her eyes were on the wastepaper basket full of discarded sheets and cigar ends. She picked it up and placed it on top of the desk.

Elizabeth continued searching the desk while Lucy rummaged through the rubbish.

It seemed like hours before Lucy gave a soft cry of victory. She beckoned to Elizabeth, and the two girls peered at the writing on a torn piece of paper. It mentioned that Lord Willoughby was in the bathtub at the time of the murder and alone. They found nothing else of significance.

"I think Lord Claybrook has kept the diary with the details of the interviews in his bedchamber," Lucy concluded. "The man is intelligent. He must have realised that everyone in the house, including the servants, would be keen to get their hands on his diary. After all, it not only has alibis but may hold a lot of family secrets."

Elizabeth nodded. Her face seemed oddly feverish.

Lucy put her agitation down to their failed attempt as well as the heightened emotions of the last hour. She headed to the door and paused when she realised Elizabeth wasn't following her. She turned back enquiringly.

"I am going to put this basket back," Elizabeth waved her on. "I won't be long."

Lucy nodded and hurried out of the room. She headed towards the dining room to signal to Master Willoughby that they were done.

Chapter Twenty

Lucy

Lucy crouched near the entrance of the dining room, trying to get Master Willoughby's attention.

Several glittering guests sat at the long wooden dining table, and Master Willoughby stood next to his father at the head of the table.

It seemed his poetry recitation was over, and he was now dancing with a candelabra. Unfortunately, the musicians in the drawing-room were playing a merry jig, while Master Willoughby was attempting a slow waltz.

Most of the guests were ignoring the boy. A few glanced at him in amusement, while others looked uncomfortable.

Lady Willoughby was trying to catch his eye, but he was studiously ignoring her.

Lord Willoughby, meanwhile, seemed oblivious of the happenings around him. He sat clutching his wine glass, looking glazed and fearful.

Surprisingly, at the other end of the table, a fully clothed Lord Aston was sleeping on top of his shredded lambchop. That is, the fact that he was fully clothed was a surprise, not that he was asleep on his dinner plate.

The table was laden with meats, soups and expensive fruits. Delicate china, polished silver and crystal glasses sparkled in the twinkling candlelight, while spring flowers woven through the serving bowls made the entire meal look even more tempting.

She eyed the table enviously, and her stomach roared in protest.

In the middle of the table sat the piece de resistance; a gorgeous wobbly pudding covered in pastel-hued candied flowers. It was a beautiful cream coloured affair that sat like a big, fat crown at the centre of the table. Dark sweet sauce trickled down its sides and flowed onto a ring of lush berries. It was the chef's masterpiece, and she could look at it forever.

Lucy's belly began to grumble loud enough for her to wonder if anyone had heard it.

The guests continued eating, none glancing her way. Even if they did spot her, they would assume she was a servant and ignore her

Suddenly Lord Aston started waking. He sneezed, mopped his face clean of brown sauce and drool, and crooked his finger at the valet.

Master Willoughby panicked as he realised what was happening; Lord Aston was about to leave the room.

Lucy's heart warmed. He didn't want anyone leaving until he got the signal. He was taking his task very seriously.

Meanwhile, Lord Aston's sozzled eyes began to move slowly towards the exit, and he pushed his chair back and lifted his arms, a signal for the valet to pick him up.

Lucy was about to flee when suddenly Master Willoughby gave a roar of desperation, leapt upon the table, pulled down his breeches and sank his bottom into the beautiful wobbly custard pudding.

The valet froze, leaving Lord Aston swinging in his grip in mid-air. The guests' mouth dropped open in horror, and Lady Willoughby let out a keening cry.

The room went silent in shock. Lucy stifled a hiccup.

Slowly the room began to stir. The young lady who had been rained upon, even though it hadn't rained in England for the last two days, swooned and landed on the carpet with a thud.

Her mother leapt up with a cry, and her old fashioned, voluminous satin skirt knocked over a candlestick setting part of the table on fire.

A servant silently and efficiently whacked the flickering flames with a cushion while the rest of the guests stared openmouthed at the breech less Master Willoughby still sitting in the middle of the table on top of the pudding.

"Can I have a berry?" the boy asked, his lashes fluttering innocently.

Lady Willoughby let out a wail that a banshee would envy. If Master Willoughby's war cry hadn't been enough warning, then this mad noise would have had the girls fleeing the study.

Master Willoughby turned just then and spotted her near the entrance.

He offered her a weak smile, and Lucy smiled back tearfully, feeling awfully proud of her little charge.

He had been magnificent today.

Chapter Twenty-One

Elizabeth

Elizabeth stood reading a letter that she had found amongst the papers on the desk.

Lucy had left not a moment ago, and she felt guilty for lying to her, but she wasn't sure if she was ready to confess her secrets just yet.

Her eyes flew over the elegant writing, her heart racing like a crazed horse.

A moment later, she was sharply spun around.

Lord Claybrook stood in front of her, his mouth twisted in anger.

She stifled a scream and hid the letter behind her back. "My lord?"

His eyes glittered as he glared down at her. He slowly reached behind her and gripped her wrist, "What are you hiding?"

Her fingers tightened on the paper turning white with the pressure. "N-nothing."

The fire in the grate spluttered and died, leaving the single candle on the desk to illuminate the room. At the same time, the musicians stopped playing, and the sudden silence made her feel as if they were the only two people in the world.

They stood in semi-darkness, so close that she could see their misty breaths mingling together.

His scent was intoxicating, a heady mix of brandy and cigar

smoke.

Suddenly, his fingers twisted her wrist.

She arched towards him in pain. "You are hurting me."

His grip gentled at once. "What are you doing here?"

"I came to get a book."

"This is not the library."

"You have some here too . . . I saw one earlier that took my fancy. I came to fetch it."

"What is the name of the book?"

Her eyes flew towards the shelves, but he tipped his head to block her view.

She froze as she realised his lips were now a breath away from hers.

They had never been this close before.

She felt his fingers hot against her wrist and became aware of the warmth emanating from his chest. A small step and she would be flush against him.

An odd languid feeling began to overtake her as if her body had softened and begun to melt. She wanted to lean into him and feel his arms enveloping her.

She felt as if she had downed a bottle of gin and turned into a shameless doxy. She no longer wanted to escape.

"You were snooping," he snapped.

She blinked in confusion. He seemed immune to the feelings spinning inside her. His face was rigid, and his eyes cold. She forced herself to focus on his words. What had he asked her?

He clicked his tongue impatiently. "What's wrong with you? Deuced woman! Answer me. What are you doing here?"

"I wanted to see if I could find any evidence against the killer," she stuttered.

"In my study? You think I killed him?"

"This is Lord Willoughby's study," she reminded him.

"I don't trust you."

She dropped her lashes. "I am speaking the truth."

"What were you reading when I came in?"

"What does it matter?" she asked, her eyes flying to his face in defiance.

His words had hurt her. The way he was looking at her now, as if she was an unwanted pest, was hurting her.

Anger rose in her, turning her blind with irrational rage. She wanted to lash out at him. She squirmed in his grip, trying to escape before she lost control.

He didn't let go.

She used her free hand to pummel him while her chest rose and fell in agitation. "Let me go."

"Not until you answer my question."

He held her easily, and her efforts became more volatile, more desperate.

He pulled her into an embrace, and she stilled.

"Will you stop fighting me?" he asked, his voice dark and husky.

She squirmed again, and he swore violently.

"Please," he bit out.

She frowned, wondering why he sounded as if he were in pain.

His hands tightened around her trim waist, and when she remained quiet, he took a step away from her. "I want to see the letter you were reading."

She shook her head, though her heart was no longer in the argument.

His eyes narrowed, and then a sensual half smile lifted the corners of his mouth.

Something changed in the air.

He slowly took in her delicate figure, her upturned face and stilled when they fell on her lips.

His eyes were warm and disturbing, like pinpricks to her soul.

His expression became heated with longing, and his hand rose to tuck a strand of stray hair behind her ear.

His fingers grazed her sensitive nape, her eyes fluttered closed, and she began to tremble.

When he stepped close to her again, she stopped breathing.

A strange excitement began surging through her, and she felt lightheaded and weak.

As if he understood, his arms went around her, and she swayed into him.

In a trice, he whipped the letter out of her hand and stepped back.

She blinked dazedly, and her pink mouth fell open in confusion.

"I didn't want to hurt you," he said. "Or take the letter by force so...." He left the rest of it unsaid.

She blushed furiously. She was ashamed of herself. Mortified at how easily she had turned into a silly, swooning wench.

"You hide a roaring fire behind that deceptive, controlled visage," he said without looking up. He read the contents of the letter and discarded it.

When she didn't respond, he said, "You could have asked me for this."

She blinked at him stupidly.

"The letter from Jane's mother, that you were reading," he clarified, his tone suddenly gentle. "You can take it with you."

"Are-are you certain?"

He shrugged. "I have no need for it."

He was so matter of fact and detached. The intensity she had felt a moment before vanished, and she wondered if she had imagined it all.

She reached towards the letter, and their fingers touched.

His eyes shot to her, and she saw startled awareness in them.

She quickly snatched the letter and fled.

She couldn't understand this violent flood of emotion. The odd power he held over her. She had wanted to please him before, but now, she wanted to kiss him.

Oh, to have his lips touch her just once, she thought as she ran down the hallway towards her room.

How was it possible to want to thwack a man and kiss him at the same time?

It was a thought that plagued her often from that day.

Chapter Twenty-Two

Lucy

The gazebo was delightfully warm. Sunlight filtered in through its tall windows, so bright that Lucy, lying on a cream bench, pulled the bonnet over her eyes. The skirt of her pale-yellow morning gown skimmed her legs and flowed over the side of the bench, exposing her ankles.

Elizabeth sat at the other end of the gazebo, her eyes unfocused and chin raised in deep thought. Her feet were primly crossed, and a bit of lace petticoat showed under her soft white muslin skirt. A parasol lay discarded by her side, while a book and a bowl of green apples sat on the bench next to her.

"What are you thinking about?" Lucy asked.

"Nothing."

"You have been staring at the cupid's statue all morning. It is sweet, but not worthy of such intense speculation."

"Not all morning. We just arrived."

"It's mid-day. The bells rang a moment ago."

"You jest!" Elizabeth exclaimed.

"What does it matter?" Lucy asked, closing her eyes again. "Morning, night or noon. We have nothing to do."

"We have a killer to catch."

Lucy sat up with a sigh. She had hoped, away from the house, Elizabeth would confess that she was not Jane, but all the blasted girl had done was daydream.

She wondered if she should tackle her to the ground and force her to confess. Playing this game of patience was becoming difficult, and one of these days, she was going to slip up and call her Elizabeth.

She stared at the girl, silently beseeching her to tell her the truth. She widened her eyes and blinked rapidly, trying to look trustworthy.

Elizabeth leaned away from her. "Are you going to cast up your accounts?"

"Eh?"

"You have turned a peculiar shade."

Lucy gave up and focused on the murder instead. "The only clue we found in the study was Lord Willoughby's alibi."

"He said he was in a bathtub." Elizabeth produced a scrap of paper from her reticule. "Not much of an alibi."

Lucy stood up and began pacing. "What do we know about Lord Willoughby?

"Surely you don't suspect him."

Lucy frowned. "I suspect everyone."

"But he was the target!" Elizabeth protested.

"Was he?"

"You mean—"

"Maybe Lord Willoughby gave Lord Beazley his clothes on purpose. He then sent him out on a wild errand, followed him and shot him. And he knew the family would assume the bullet had been meant for him."

"But the reason the family thinks the bullet was meant for Lord Willoughby is that no one had a motive to kill Beazley. No one knew him well enough."

"Lord Willoughby did."

Elizabeth's eyes widened. "So, he did."

"How do you know they were not enemies?"

Elizabeth jumped up and joined Lucy in a languid stroll. "Lord Willoughby could have secretly hated the man."

Lucy nodded. "He could have caught Lady Willoughby and Beazley in a compromising position. It is entirely possible considering the woman is miserable in her marriage and has shamelessly flirted with every man that has come to Gopshall. She didn't even spare the poor butler."

Elizabeth paused at an old, dry fountain. She eyed the two stone fishes almost kissing over a marble basin and frowned, "I just remembered something. Lady Willoughby had been in love with Claybrook before she married Lord Willoughby."

"Truly?" Lucy caught Elizabeth's arm and spun her to search her face. "Lord Willoughby knew about this?"

Elizabeth nodded. "I heard it from Lord Claybrook's housekeeper. Lord Claybrook had agreed to marry Lady Willoughby. They were betrothed. But Claybrook had not inherited his aunt's wealth or title at the time, so Lady Willoughby decided to marry his elder brother instead, a widower with three children. Lord Claybrook went on to marry a close friend who died a few years later in an accident."

"Why would Lord Willoughby agree to marry his brother's betrothed?"

"Perhaps he loved her too. She is beautiful, after all."

Lucy raised her eyebrow sceptically. "But to hurt his own brother so?"

"Spite. Lord Willoughby has always been jealous of Lord Claybrook. Claybrook, despite being the younger son, has always commanded far more respect, not only from society but also his family. His mother doted on him."

"We may be onto something here," Lucy mused. "Lord Claybrook is handsome, charming and intelligent. Lord Willoughby is . . . well, a bit of a blob. A blob that knows his wife despises him. She married him for his title while she was in love with his brother. That must hurt. And Lord Aston treating him like a farce is bound to hurt him even more."

"Perhaps, he is hiding a bitter, malevolent, heart behind that pathetic, helpless mask?" Elizabeth mused.

"True. No one likes him . . . which is why the family easily believed that he was the target. He gambles, drinks, and chases skirts. The servants don't speak fondly of him either."

Elizabeth poked a bit of mud with her parasol. "I recall one more thing. This was a few months ago before you had arrived at Gopshall. It's gossip and I can't be certain, but I remember the servants discussing the fact that it was odd that the three men Lord Willoughby had gambled with in the past, and lost a fair bit to, had—"

"Yes?"

"They had mysteriously died. But Lord Willoughby had an excellent alibi every single time."

Lucy whistled. "I believe Lord Willoughby has suddenly become our main suspect."

"But . . . it could be hearsay."

"An odd sort of hearsay that comes true months later. A fourth man who was gambling with Willoughby suddenly ends up dead."

Elizabeth clutched herself as if suddenly cold. "It's awful talking about people like that, isn't it? I will never be able to look at Lord Willoughby the same again."

Lucy rubbed her arms and nodded. "People are strange, Miss Peyton."

"Does this mean you will abandon the idea of following the butler?"

"We still don't know who killed him. This is just speculation. A neat theory, but we need proof. The butler could have done it too. We can't give up on anyone yet."

"I think it's too dangerous," Elizabeth said stubbornly. "You could get hurt."

"I am going to wait until he leaves the house and then search his room.

"I am going to help you."

"I can't let you. He almost killed me."

"We are in this together, and I want to help you. Besides, it will be harder for him to kill two governesses than one."

Lucy hugged her impulsively. "Thank you. Now, all we have to do is wait for the man to leave."

∞∞∞

Elizabeth

Early the next morning, Elizabeth donned her most comfortable dress and pocketed a few biscuits, a paring knife, a small rope, and a letter from her beloved sisters for courage.

She was ready to spy.

The day promised to be awful; clouds hung thick and dark in the sky and the soft, gentle breeze of yesterday had morphed into a roaring gale. Gopshall Manor creaked and wheezed in the forceful winds as if it was tired of all the theatrics going on inside and outside the manor.

She spotted her target the moment she emerged from her bedchamber. The butler was walking a few paces ahead of her. He turned right, and she hurried after him, feeling anxious. She had never done this sort of thing before.

The butler was heading towards the kitchen, she realised and forced herself to slow down and walk at a measured pace.

The butler glanced back just then, and she politely nodded to him.

He smiled back and continued his way.

She had every right to head in the same direction as him, and yet, a trickle of fear stayed with her. What if he guessed her motive was not to have a cup of tea but to keep an eye on him?

She caught a glimpse of herself in a small mirror hanging on the landing and paused. Her hair was tied in a neat bun. Her cream, speckled muslin dress was clean if a little faded with age. It skimmed her curves and felt soft and comfortable against her skin. Her face, dusted with light freckles, appeared calm and confident.

It seemed that her pretending to be someone else this past

year had taught her how to mask her feelings and appear in control even if she was trembling inside.

She turned away from her reflection and took a deep breath, ready to trail the butler once more, when Lord Claybrook's low, angry voice coming from the music room made her pause and tilt her head.

She watched the butler disappear down the hallway and frowned. She wanted to follow the butler, and yet, Lord Claybrook's tone and the fact that he was in the abandoned music room made her incredibly curious. Who in the world was he talking to?

She debated for a moment and then realised that it was best to hear what Claybrook had to say. It wasn't often he used that tone and to leave a chance of gleaning vital information to follow the butler who may be simply going to have a meal would be foolish.

She inched towards the door and stuck her ear to the wood. The voices were muffled, but if she concentrated hard enough, she could make out some of the words.

"Will you stop this foolishness?" Lord Claybrook demanded.

"I am his father. I can do what I like."

"But he is delicate."

Lord Aston snorted. "Then he needs to toughen up. I have let him behave like a frightened mare for too long. He is my heir; he needs to behave like it. I am sick of the snivelling idiot."

"Someone tried to kill him. Show some compassion."

"Would you be squirrelled away in your room surrounded by pastries and sweetmeats had you been the target?"

"I am not William."

"I wish you were," Lord Aston sighed. "My days are numbered, and I *must* do something to make him change and take his responsibilities seriously. Our family name is becoming a source of amusement for the *ton*. I can't let that happen."

"But this method of yours is ridiculous. He will learn nothing from being repeatedly frightened. You are behaving like a child."

"I don't know what else to do." The defeat in Lord Aston's voice broke Elizabeth's heart.

"You can begin by not smoking disgusting cigars and live a little longer."

"What?"

"We all know the valet buys them for you, and this is where you choose to hide and smoke them. Father, we are not as foolish as you think."

"You are not foolish, but your brother and his sauce box wife have nothing in their heads."

Elizabeth heard the chair scrape back, and she quickly stepped away and headed towards the kitchen, once again. The mystery of what Lord Aston had been doing in the music room the last time when he found Lucy with the butler and Lady Willoughby, was solved. But the larger puzzle still lay scattered with plenty of the pieces missing.

The cook was stirring the pot when she walked into the kitchen. The woman briefly glanced at her and Elizabeth stifled a gasp.

The cook looked miserable. Her eyes were red-rimmed, her hair was a tangled mess, and her expression was grim.

An odd sort of tension sat in the air. She looked around and realised that the only other person in the room was the butler and from his set face it was clear that she had walked in on an argument.

Rather than defuse the situation, she wanted the tension to grow, so she grabbed a dry, wrinkled apple from the bowl on the table and strolled out of the room as quickly as she could. She left the kitchen door slightly open.

She walked down the hallway, waited a few moments and then doubled back, soft-footed, and hid behind the kitchen door. She was rewarded soon enough when the cook began speaking in a trembling voice.

"I didn't kill him. And Lady Willoughby is bound to recall it soon enough. I will tell her everything. Including your secrets and I know plenty of them."

"You haven't paid me this week, cook," the butler responded unperturbed.

"And I refuse to pay you. I have to feed and clothe my girls."

"If I remind Lady Willoughby that four years ago, the person who recommended you to her was Lord Beazley, then you will be hanging by the noose within a week."

"I worked for his mother, not him."

"That's no defence."

"I don't have the money," the cook's voice broke. "Please, you have known me for years. I would never kill anyone."

"I know nothing of the sort," the butler said, in the same calm, cold voice. "Have the money ready by the time I come back for dinner. I am going to the market to buy some ribbons for a sweetheart."

"Where will I get the money?" the cook cried.

"Steal it."

Elizabeth didn't wait to hear more and sped back up the stairs to look for Lucy. She found the girl writing letters in her room. Within moments, she had told her all she had learned.

"You are a natural," Lucy said, her eyes wide in shock. "I cannot believe you discovered so much so quickly."

"The butler is leaving now. We can head over to his room and search it," Elizabeth tugged her hand.

"Wait a few moments. The man is going to take some time getting dressed before heading out. Besides, dinner is a good while yet."

Elizabeth bounced from foot to foot. She felt as if she could solve the crime right at that moment. All they needed to do was hurry. But Lucy was right. They had to be cautious. She never knew when her luck would run out.

Chapter Twenty-Three

Lucy

It was time to search the butler's room, and Lucy could delay it no more.

It had been her idea all along, and yet, her stomach churned uneasily. She felt a wave of terror and nausea wash over her as she slowly walked behind Elizabeth towards the butler's room.

The image of the butler's hand gripping her throat kept intruding into her brain, and no matter how much she tried to divert her mind, fear continued to keep pace with her.

She glanced at Elizabeth, who appeared a little wild-eyed. Her success this morning had given her a look of a sozzled woman. Even her smooth, tame hair seemed to have frizzed in excitement.

They reached the basement in the east wing and paused. Two wooden doors stood adjacent to each other. One was butler's and the other the valet's.

"Do you know which room is his?" Lucy whispered nervously.

Elizabeth nodded. "The right one is butler's."

"How do you know?"

Elizabeth blushed. "When I had just arrived at Gopshall, he had asked me to join him."

"In his room?"

She nodded, turning redder. "I turned down his advances."

Lucy waggled her eyebrows. "Aren't you full of secrets and surprises."

Elizabeth's face fell, and Lucy bit her lip in consternation. She quickly grabbed the doorknob on her right and opened the door.

The butler's uniform was draped over a chair in the corner.

She heaved a sigh of relief which soon turned into a cough as an awful stench hit her at the back of her throat.

"What is that smell?" she spluttered.

Elizabeth wrinkled her nose. "The bitter aroma of a bachelor's lodgings."

Lucy peered around the room with watery eyes and her brows slowly rose in horror. She wasn't very neat herself, but this . . . this was shocking.

The room was reasonably large. It had a bed, not a murphy to be let down like hers, but a proper bed, a desk, a chair and a window that opened.

The bed was unmade, stained and stank like it had never been changed. A tray with bits of old bread, cheese and meat sat where the pillow should have been.

The wooden floor was strewn with dirty socks, snuff stained gloves, handkerchiefs, tobacco leaves, and mouldy apple cores.

The desk contained oil, wax, ink, broken pens, parchment, combs, a few shirts and a pile of ribbons. A travelling box was stuffed under the desk, while a washstand stood in a corner next to a thin wardrobe.

Lucy nodded towards the washstand, "That pitcher will do nicely."

Elizabeth frowned. "The pitcher?"

"To hit the butler on the head with, if he walks in on us."

"Oh. Do you want me to hold it?"

"Like your life depends on it," Lucy responded, soberly.

"We could tie him up in those tobacco-stained curtains afterwards and dump his body in the forest."

"We are not going to kill him!"

"Why ever not? We are going to be blamed for Mr Beazley's

murder anyway, so we might as well do some good and kill a man who deserves it. One murder or twenty, we can be hung only once. Also, if we kill him, we will be protecting the women of England from an awful creature."

"Jane?"

"Yes?"

"You have gone mad."

"Perhaps, you are right."

"Calm your blood lust. Its broad daylight, not a full moon night."

"As you say."

"Can we focus on searching the room now?"

Elizabeth clutched the pitcher to her chest and took her position by the door. "I shall keep guard."

Lucy began searching the desk. She found nothing apart from a whole lot of beeswax candles. She naturally snuck a few into her pocket. How did the man manage to obtain so many expensive candles?

"Lady Willoughby must have given them to him, or he keeps some, every time he buys them for Gopshall," Elizabeth said.

Lucy moved on to the wardrobe. She found a box of lurid love letters. She read a few bits out to Elizabeth who heard it all in horrified fascination.

"Here is another," Lucy giggled. "Oh, to have your fingertips tickle my upper lip. I long for you my beloved butler. I am your very own fish guttler."

"Guttler?" Elizabeth chuckled.

Lucy pulled yet another letter out of the box. "My beloved, you have won, and I am wooed. I have attached a lock of my hair, as you requested. It may smell faintly of cows since I have been with them all morning."

Elizabeth snorted in response.

Lucy picked up a crumpled piece of paper on the floor and smoothed it open. "This one is from the butler," she said squinting at the writing. "It simply says, 'To my sweetheart. I can barely contain my thrill at realising that you love me. The moment I see you, I will kiss you until I kill you.'"

Elizabeth shuddered. "Frightening."

Lucy moved the box and peered deeper into the wardrobe. "He has a few more love letters, portraits of eyes of various women, locks of hair, bottles of gin, oh, and a baby mouse."

"I hear footsteps," Elizabeth warned.

Lucy snuck a few letters into her already bulging pockets. She had a feeling the butler used these to blackmail several girls.

"Hurry," Elizabeth urged, her voice a touch shrill with anxiety.

Lucy leapt over a pair of boots and reached for the doorknob. It flew open before she touched it.

It was the butler.

He gripped her neck before she could take in what happened.

"Nosing are we?" he growled. His other hand shot out and hit Elizabeth on her shoulder before she could bring the pitcher down on him. She fell to the ground with a cry of pain.

Lucy's eyes bulged as she struggled to breath.

Elizabeth scrabbled back up, clutching her arm. She breathed in sharply, leapt upon the butler's back and sank her teeth into his shoulder, forcing him to release his hold on Lucy.

Lucy wheezed and stumbled towards the door. The butler grabbed the back of her dress, and she felt the fabric rip.

At the same time, he threw Elizabeth off his back and turned to face her.

"Stop."

The command made everyone freeze. Lucy's heart leapt in hope as she slowly lifted her lashes and looked towards the door.

A sudden stiff breeze whipped the house cap off her head. Her hair fell in loose waves around her face, and her eyes grew large and wide.

In front of her stood Lord William Hartell Adair, the most handsome man in England.

The breeze gentled and caressed his hair, while the long blue coat swirled about his legs. His eyes, so sharp and heavily fringed with dark lashes, swept over her, they narrowed when they spotted fingerprints on her neck and the state of her dress.

He glanced towards the butler, and she trembled at the expression in his eyes.

Lord Adair's spoke softly. "I had warned you, Underhill."

"They were in my room," he spluttered. "They attacked me."

"I find that hard to believe," he drawled.

Lucy gasped, just then, as her throat burned in pain. Her vision became blurry.

Adair glanced at her in concern. "Out," he snapped at the butler.

The butler scrambled out as fast as he could.

"You are letting him go?" Elizabeth asked. "He almost killed us."

"He will get what he deserves," Adair replied, his eyes on Lucy. He stepped towards her and held out his hand.

The world slowed, and Lucy burst into tears.

She didn't know why she began howling like a forlorn pup, but she did. In a trice, she flung herself into his arms, and he held her close.

"I did not think you would return," she wailed. "But you did. Oh, thank goodness, you did."

All these days, she had fought bravely, kept control of her emotions and suffered a hostile environment with a smile on her face. It was hard seeing bitter, angry glances thrown her way. Even Elizabeth didn't trust her enough to share her secrets.

She felt as if she had been wading through mud and slime trying to keep her head above the water. She had to prove her innocence, find the murderer, and keep herself safe from the likes of Lady Willoughby and the butler. And Adair, her anchor, had disappeared, leaving her adrift on a sea of questions.

He held her through her crying fit. He spoke not a word but let her regain her composure.

She finally stopped hiccupping and stepped back from him.

He handed her a snowy white handkerchief, his eyes carefully averted.

She looked down and realised that her stays had come loose, and her morning dress had slipped off one shoulder, exposing the soft rise of her breast. She blushed and turned away from him.

She yanked her sleeve up, mopped her face and looked around to find Elizabeth had vanished. She wasn't surprised since her outburst would have frightened any sensible girl. She dropped her lashes, unable to look at Lord Adair or explain herself. She felt like a fool, a child who had yet to learn how to tame her wild emotions.

"Have you finished blubbering?" Adair finally asked, in a bored tone.

"I am sorry."

"It is not the first time a woman has thrown herself at me, my dear."

"I did not throw myself at you."

"You bounded into my arms like an eager rabbit."

"I was relieved to see you."

He shrugged, "Whatever the reason, you did hop into my arms."

"I hopped like a forlorn, lost baby bird who has seen her mother ... not like a damsel who has spied her knight."

"You think of me like a mother bird?"

"A comforting hen," she nodded.

He suddenly smiled, and she was momentarily blinded by the smile. He didn't look like a hen just then . . . but the delicious, sensual man he was.

She shook her head and stepped back. He must have a dozen women sobbing on his shoulder every week. She had heard some swooned just by looking at him . . . she had no need to be embarrassed. Everyone knew he had a strong effect on some men and women.

"Tell me all that you have discovered," he said, taking off his coat and laying it on her shoulders to hide the state of her dress.

She clutched the deep blue fabric gratefully, feeling its warmth spread through her bones.

His brisk, unconcerned tone helped her regain her composure, and she began filling him in about all she and Elizabeth had learned.

By the time he had walked her back to her room, she was feeling like her cheerful self again.

Chapter Twenty-Four

Elizabeth

Elizabeth felt guilty for abandoning Lucy, but the way she had been sobbing on Lord Adair's shoulder, she had to leave. The moment had been intimate, and she doubted Lucy wanted to be seen in such a vulnerable state.

She grabbed her parasol and headed out to look for Lucy now and explain herself. It was a sunny day, and she wondered if the sky had cheered up with Lord Adair's arrival.

Lord Adair, the man, was . . . easy to love. She frowned, her heart did not beat wildly in his presence, but she knew if she spent a few days with him, she would be swooning in front of him like most of England.

She headed towards the kitchen, her thoughts heavy. Lucy had lived a sheltered life in the orphanage. She had grown up surrounded by women and was even more naïve than a country girl like her. Her poor, chaste heart would never stand a chance against a man like Adair.

Soon enough, Adair would seep into her soul and enchant her. She would fall madly in love and then be miserable for the rest of her life since she would never be able to find another man good enough in comparison.

Adair was like a bottle of sugared arsenic. The more time Lucy spent with him, the deeper she would fall in love, and then, perhaps, never recover from the subsequent heartbreak.

Sure, Lucy was lovely in a wild sort of way, and any man would be lucky to have her, but she was an orphan and he . . . the Marquess of Lockwood.

She supposed, Adair was sensible enough to understand that his kindness could be misconstrued by Lucy, and he would do his best to keep his distance from her. Perhaps, that's why he had stayed away for so long and left the investigation in Claybrook's hands.

"It's raining. You don't need the parasol."

Elizabeth blinked in surprise, "I was just thinking about you."

Lucy grinned, "Ah, so I have finally charmed you. Confess, my dear, you adore me now. My presence makes your heart flutter, and when I leave, you pine like a forlorn fisherwoman whose husband is lost at sea."

"You are like a mouse," she shook her head and chuckled. "A baby mouse that will bring the plague upon my head one day, but for the moment I can't help but coo over its tiny form."

"Speaking of love," Lucy waggled her eyebrows, "I see the way you look at Claybrook."

"Hush!! she growled. "Someone will hear you."

"Ah, so you admit you love him."

"I am sorry for abandoning you in the butler's room—"

"You are forgiven. Now, let's get back to the subject you are avoiding. Claybrook."

"I have to give Master Willoughby this meat pie to thank him for helping us earlier—"

"Janey loves Claybrook, Janey loves Claybrook—"

A throat cleared behind them, and Elizabeth gasped. "C-Claybrook?"

Lucy turned bright red. "I was only jesting."

Claybrook cocked his head. "Jesting about what?"

Elizabeth sighed in relief. He hadn't heard.

"I wanted to speak to you, Miss Trotter."

Lucy shuffled backwards, "Later. I mean, I have to be somewhere."

"It will only take a moment."

"I have to go," she insisted.

Elizabeth frowned, why was she acting so strange suddenly "Lucy?"

Lucy started walking very fast.

Elizabeth exchanged a worried glance with Claybrook. Was the girl ill?

They sped after her.

Lucy began running.

"We can help," Elizabeth responded. "Stop, a moment. What's the matter?"

"Nothing, go away!"

Claybrook grabbed Lucy's arm outside the nursery and halted her. "Why are you running, Miss Trotter?"

The nursery door opened, and Master Willoughby poked his head out. "What's going on?"

"Lucy? Trust us." Elizabeth urged.

A soft sound filled the air.

Claybrook frowned. "What was that?"

"I-I sneezed," Lucy responded red-faced.

Claybrook frowned, and then his eyes widened in under-standing. "That, Miss Trotter, does not smell like a sneeze."

"I have stinky sneezes," Lucy mumbled under her breath.

"Good lord," Claybrook wheezed. "It's so bad, you made Johnny cry."

Master Willoughby wiped his tears and bowed to Lucy. "Madam, that was magnificent. May I know what you ate for dinner?"

Lucy closed her eyes and whispered in mortification. "Beans and cabbage. Ghastly beans and cabbage."

∞ ∞ ∞

Elizabeth and Claybrook tactfully allowed Lucy to escape and began walking back towards the drawing-room.

"What did you want to ask Lucy?" Elizabeth spoke to break

the silence.

"I wanted to know if she knew when Lord Adair will be back."

"We met him this afternoon."

"He left soon after. I hoped Lucy knew when he would return. She was the last person to speak to him."

"He is extremely busy, isn't he?" she asked, stepping inside the drawing-room.

"No one is here," Claybrook remarked vaguely, his eyes darting hither thither.

She knew his expression well. Something was bothering him.

"Did you mean it?" he suddenly burst out.

She frowned. "Mean what?"

"That you are in love with me."

Her eyes widened. "You heard us!"

He waited for her to continue.

"I didn't mean it," she quickly assured the carpet.

"Look at me and say it."

She moved her eyeballs towards the snuffbox lying on the table. Her lids felt heavy, refusing to rise any higher. "What do you care?"

He caught her chin and lifted it up. "Look at me, Miss Verney."

She jerked her chin away from his clasp. "No! I refuse to do your bidding. I am no longer employed by you, so you can no longer order me about. I am not a puppet, and you are not my puppeteer. I just want to find the murderer and get away from you."

"*You* want to find the murderer?" he asked, his voice laced with amusement.

"I can. I have found out a lot in the past few days," she snapped.

"I think you should stop interfering," he narrowed his eyes.

"Why?"

"It's dangerous."

"I am fed up," she turned away from him. "I am tired of being a frightened mouse. They blame me anyway, so better I die trying to prove my innocence than be led like an old, obedient horse to its end."

He gripped her shoulder and swung her around. "I said, leave it alone. If you are innocent, then I will do my best to prove it."

"Did you not hear a word I said? I no longer do your bidding. I am no longer your children's governess. And if you want to find out the truth, then help me, not deter me."

"It's not a woman's business."

"A woman can murder but not search for clues to prove her innocence?" she cried.

He closed his eyes, looking pained. "Fine, what do you want to know?"

"Please tell me where the butler was on the morning of the murder?"

He stared down at her; his expression torn. "He doesn't have an alibi," he finally admitted.

She thoughtlessly placed her hand on his chest and smiled up at him. She was elated that he had shared the information with her. Perhaps, he *did* believe that she hadn't killed Beazley.

He seemed stunned at her sudden boldness. His eyes widened in shock.

Her own expression changed to horror when she realised that she was gripping his shirt, and her knuckles were grazing his neck.

His hand shot out and grabbed her waist before she could flee.

"You have never smiled at me before," he said huskily.

She squirmed in his grip. "I am sorry . . . I . . . I have to go."

"Nay, not yet," he said, his eyes turning dark and turbulent.

She felt his warmth invade her bones, and she stilled.

His head dipped, and he searched her face. "I am tired of play-ing this game with you."

Her mouth trembled, and she bit her lip to steady herself. "W-what game?"

"Are you attracted to me, Elizabeth?"

Her eyes widened and flew to his. "I-I don't know what you mean."

"You know precisely what I mean," he growled.

His eyes were flashing in anger, and his face was inscrutable as if carved out of stone and yet, his fingers tenderly tucked a strand of hair behind her ears.

She closed her eyes and leaned her cheek against his palm. Her breathing became laboured, and her chest rose and fell in agitation.

"Will, you not confess, Lizzy?"

Her lashes flickered open, and she stared at him, her eyes full of emotion.

The dinner gong rang, breaking the fragile moment, and they sprang apart.

Her mind did not ask inane questions like what was happening to her? It did not question the feelings swirling inside her like a storm. She knew what they were, like she knew her own name.

She was in love with him.

She came alive around him; the fire burned hotter, the wind blew colder, and fabrics felt softer against her skin.

The sensual scent of damask roses lying on the mantlepiece teased her senses, and for a moment, she felt an urge to confess.

But what good would it do to tell him how she felt? He would never marry her, and she could settle for nothing else.

If she did tell him, he would pity her, and that would be worse than being accused of a murder.

He cleared his throat, and she looked up to find he was watching her. Watching the expressions flitting across her face. Could he read them?

She curled her fingers into a fist lest they begin to smooth the lines on his forehead, stroke his hair, or gently push him into the chair.

She wanted to bring him a plate of dinner, a warm whisky and his house slippers. She wanted to hear all he had done that day, what had made him laugh, what had made him worry. She wanted to know everything about him, his mind, his heart, his feelings.

She tried to hold on to this moment. To commit every detail

to memory, for when she left, it was all she would have of him.

His voice was low and thick when he spoke. "I have to go."

She nodded, still unable to speak. Love, it seemed, had tip-toed into her heart and stolen her tongue.

Chapter Twenty-Five

Lucy

"Lord Adair wants to talk to us," Lucy said, grabbing Elizabeth's hand and pulling her into the library.

The library was one of the biggest rooms in the house. It had a few shelves full of dusty books with ornate spines procured more for show than reading.

A large sandalwood cabinet standing next to the window had beautiful gilt jars filled with all sorts of snuff, snuff boxes and liquor.

The wooden desk, doors, and the ornate skirtings were made of polished mahogany, while the chairs and curtains were blue velvet. An entire wall facing the window was covered in mirrors, capturing the outdoors like paintings on canvases.

Lord Adair sat by the fire, reading a book bound in dark red leather. He wore a luxurious gold and green robe that made his features look even more regal than usual. His eyes sparkled when he saw them approach.

"Tell me everything you have learned," he said, setting aside his book.

Lucy bobbed a curtsy. "We think the butler did it."

"Why?"

"He tried to kill me," she replied.

"I admit, I have wanted to throttle you myself a few times," Lord Adair mused. "But, Miss Trotter, many people *try* to kill.

It's the ones who go through with it that end up being criminals."

Elizabeth stepped forward. "He is having an affair with Lady Willoughby."

Lord Adair shrugged unimpressed.

Lucy frowned. "Maybe Beazley spotted the butler and Lady Willoughby canoodling?

"Or they wanted to get rid of Lord Willoughby," Elizabeth put in.

He leaned back in his chair and eyed the girls. "Sit," he said, gesturing towards the chairs facing him.

They sat; their bottoms perched on the very edge of the seat.

He steepled his fingers together and spoke thoughtfully, "If they got rid of Willoughby, the title and the house would go to Claybrook. Lady Willoughby would lose much of the wealth and her station. Claybrook might raise Master Willoughby as his heir, but that would depend on the kindness of his future wife. As for Beazley spotting them together, what good would it have done? I think Lord Willoughby knows far more than he lets on. He has known about his wife's indiscretions for some time. She doesn't try to hide it."

"But the butler has no alibi," the girls cried.

"He does," Lord Adair corrected them. "He was with the maid; Mary, I think her name is. He did not want Lady Willoughby to know, so he kept the fact hidden. Mary confessed it all to me."

Lucy's mouth fell open.

"But Lord Claybrook said he doesn't have an alibi," Elizabeth argued.

Lord Adair smiled. "I have been doing this for a long time, my dear. Lord Claybrook is an honest man. He never thinks to doubt or suspect. If you tell him your name is Jane, then he will believe you."

Lucy felt the shift in the atmosphere. The air became tense, and Elizabeth's hands began to shake, so she caught them between her own and swiftly changed the topic. "When did you speak to Mary? I thought you had left the questioning to Lord

Claybrook."

"I had a chat with everyone before I left. I let them think that Claybrook would be asking the tough questions, while I was only concerned about their wellbeing. Naturally, they stopped seeing me as a threat and let a few bits slip. Claybrook received a more guarded response."

"You tricked him," Elizabeth exploded. Lucy squeezed her hand in warning.

He shook his head and said gently, "On the contrary, he was aware of the situation from the very beginning. He has done a remarkable job."

Lucy felt Elizabeth relax next to her, and she breathed a sigh of relief. She wanted to ask him so many questions, but that would defeat her purpose. She had to reach the truth on her own and impress Adair.

She stood up and yanked Elizabeth to her feet. The girl was deathly pale and trembling like a cold kitten.

"We appreciate your help," Lucy said, to him. "If we learn anything more, we will come straight to you."

He didn't seem pleased at the prospect of seeing her again; rather, his expression appeared resigned.

"I will present you with the murderer soon," Lucy continued.

He laughed.

"I will," she insisted.

Elizabeth grabbed her arm and dragged her out of the room, leaving Lord Adair in fits of mirth.

Lucy collapsed on her bed and stared at the ceiling. "I was certain it was the butler, Mr Underhill. He is awful at his job but a charmer. Flirts shamelessly and is a bit young to be a butler. He is Lady Willoughby's lover, and is blackmailing the cook and countless other women. He is a crook and a blackguard. He is just the sort of man who would kill impulsively and never regret it."

Elizabeth lay down next to her and copied her pose. "Lord Willoughby, the butler, and even the cook are suspects. Anyone could have done it."

"Don't forget the valet, Lady Willoughby, who could have been acting on her own or . . . Claybrook."

Elizabeth sat up with a frown. "Claybrook? But Lord Adair trusts him."

Lucy shook her head and said carefully, "He was given a job. That does not prove his innocence or the fact that Adair trusts him."

"Why would he try to kill his own brother?" Elizabeth asked, her voice a touch shrill.

"You told me that he was once betrothed to Lady Willoughby. Perhaps, he was angry that his brother married her instead. He was simply waiting for the right time to make his move—"

Elizabeth shot to her feet. "He is an honourable man. He would never do anything so awful."

"He had an argument with Beazley the evening before the murder. Your feelings are clouding your judgement—"

"And you have turned into a cold-hearted creature who eyes everyone with suspicion and refuses to see the good in anyone."

"Jane—"

"Good evening, Miss Trotter," Elizabeth snapped and strode out of the room.

Lucy slapped her head in frustration and let out a moan. Wasn't it just like her to alienate the only friend she had? Oh, why did she have to open her big mouth?

Chapter Twenty-Six

Elizabeth

Elizabeth sat in the drawing-room, along with the rest of the household.

The curtains had been pulled back to let in plenty of light, and the table was laden with food as if the family had come together to celebrate a wonderful occasion, rather than listen to a grim lecture from Lord Adair.

Lord Adair stood before them in a long black coat that flowed around him like a powerful sorcerer. His hand was curled around the walking stick with the silver cheetah head, and his pale face glowed eerily.

Elizabeth didn't know if it was some sort of trick of the light, but his usual gentle appearance had been replaced with a cold, frightening demeanour.

They were seeing a side of him that people rarely witnessed. The affable, charming and slightly aloof man was gone; instead, an intelligent, all-knowing creature stood before them.

He was no longer the man that women swooned over, but the sort that made men cower.

His piercing gaze searched the faces before him, noting every flicker of expression and movement. She felt as if he was delving deep into their souls and wrenching out every secret.

She shrank in her seat when his eyes fell on her. His gaze softened and turned sympathetic, while her face warmed in mortification.

She dropped her lashes, unable to look at him. He knew who she was. She didn't know how, but he knew. And his pity troubled her.

She felt a sudden wave of revulsion overcome her. She was tired of living a lie, cheating people and despising herself. She wanted this guilt, misery and self-loathing to end.

Lord Adair's voice rang out, clear and articulate slicing through her dark thoughts.

"It's all over the papers. The gossip columns are full of it. Word has reached the prince, and he is fascinated by the murder, just like the rest of England. They want to know what happened."

"This is a disaster," Lord Aston exclaimed.

"Some of the things being said are scandalous," Lady Willoughby complained. "They think I have run away with the coachman after killing my lover."

Lord Adair tapped his walking stick for silence. "They also call you a blooming rose who is far prettier than a lot of debutantes today."

Lady Willoughby relaxed in her seat. "Oh, I wouldn't know," she said, trying to blush.

No one was fooled by her outraged innocent act.

"Thieves," Lord Adair continued, "want a piece of Beazley's corpse to sell to the public. I heard he had not a toenail left by the time he was buried."

"We have placed some men to guard the grave," Lord Claybrook commented. "We also caught some village lads trying to sneak into this house to steal souvenirs since the murder occurred here."

Lord Adair waited until the murmur of disgust and anger subsided in the room. "Lord Beazley's mother is infuriated. She is demanding Lord Willoughby and Lord Aston's heads; she wants them pickled in a jar so she can keep it in her curio cupboard."

"This is madness," Lord Aston cried. "In my day, no one would think of putting the noose around an aristocrat's head."

"Times are changing," Lord Adair replied. "The regent's conduct is being ridiculed, and people are fast losing respect for the aristocracy. The sacrifices they made for the war have further left them poor and bitter, and they hold no love for those with blue blood."

"They are like hounds," Lord Willoughby whispered from the corner. "They want to sniff us out and maul us to death."

A silence fell in the room. The family realised that they were surrounded by servants and outnumbered.

Lord Adair sank into a chair. His tone gentled, "We need to find the murderer. Things are spiralling out of control. The regent has promised not to interfere with the investigations, but I cannot vouch for Lord Pennyworth or Lord Grey. Both are old rivals of your family, and they have scented blood. They are trying their best to oust Lord Willoughby from Parliament and malign the Willoughby reputation."

"Liars!" Lord Aston exploded. "Both the men are liars. Lord Pennyworth is a mushroom, while Lord Grey has lived his life on other people's charity."

Lord Adair took a sip of wine. "They say Willoughby lost Gopshall to Lord Grey's son during a gambling session."

"What foolishness!" Lord Aston exploded. "They have no witnesses, no proof."

"They say that shortly after Willoughby lost, someone stole the proof," Lord Adair replied.

Lord Willoughby shrank deeper into his chair as all eyes swung towards him.

"I detest liars," Lady Willoughby pouted. "Disgusting dishonourable creatures."

Elizabeth felt the words hit home. It didn't matter who had said it, but it was like a slap in the face.

"Miss Peyton," Claybrook said. "the cup is going to fall."

Elizabeth stared at the china cup tilting dangerously in her hand. His tone had been mocking when he had used her assumed name.

A moment later, the cup slipped from her fingers, and the cup fell with a thud on the rose carpet splashing tea everywhere.

"You, *numbskull!*" Lady Willoughby cried, while Mary swiftly pulled out a rag and began mopping up the mess.

"I have something to confess," Elizabeth sprang up, her tone was tight with emotion.

"Miss Peyton," Claybrook's tone held a warning.

She looked at him then, her eyes beseeching him to let her confess. The lie was eating her up.

He shook his head slightly. His eyes were dark and worried.

"Did you kill Beazley? Is that what you want to confess?" Lord Willoughby sat up eagerly.

"I knew it!" Lady Willoughby crowed.

Elizabeth took a deep breath and spoke in a rush. "I didn't kill him. But I did lie about my identity. My name is not Jane Peyton. It is Elizabeth Verney. I was a friend of Jane's and was with her when she breathed her last. She asked me to take her position as the governess for Lord Claybrook since she knew I needed it. I agreed, and here I am."

"I can't believe this," the cook gasped, forgetting her place for a moment.

"I am a liar and a fraud," Elizabeth's voice trembled.

"Miss Verney," Lord Adair's gentle tone undid her.

She left the room before others could witness her tears. She walked blindly, her eyes on the floor.

A hand gripped her elbow and dragged her into a room.

The door slammed shut behind her, and she didn't care. She didn't care where she was or with whom.

The enormity of what she had done began sinking in.

"You little idiot," Claybrook glared at her. "What a foolish thing to do! You have just made yourself the prime suspect in the case."

"I know," she whispered miserably. "But I couldn't go on lying. I would rather have the noose around my neck—"

He placed a finger on her lips, "Nay, you would rather live."

"Oh, what do you care? It is my decision."

"Shh, someone will hear you. And we just happen to be in my

room, unchaperoned."

She wrenched her arm away from him. "Damn propriety. I don't care about anything anymore."

His hand shot out and caught her waist. "I said, keep your voice down. If you don't care about your reputation, think about mine."

"I didn't ask you to chase after me."

"Elizabeth," he snapped angrily. "You are making one mistake after another. You need to calm down and be sensible."

"I have no sense," she said, trying to escape his grip. "I am full of silly notions and feelings. You keep your sense and let me live with my sensibility."

He tightened his grip around her waist and yanked her forward until she was flush against him. "If you will not think of yourself, then I will have to do it for you."

Her eyes widened as his head dipped, and his lips claimed hers in a possessive kiss.

When the kiss ended, her eyes were glazed, and it took her a moment to find her feet. She lifted her lashes and discovered his face was filled with shock at what he had done.

Her heart broke at the horror on his face, and she quickly stepped away. Neither spoke as she exited the room.

Chapter Twenty-Seven

Lucy

Lucy paused outside the library door. "Err, Jane, I mean, Elizabeth, what are you doing?"

Elizabeth cleared her throat. "I was hoping to eavesdrop and find some information about the murder."

"Ah, and you need to hang on the back of the door to accomplish this?"

"I thought it was a good idea."

"The door is solid mahogany, and unlike the study, extremely thick. You wouldn't be able to hear a thing."

"Maybe it's thinner at the top."

"For a person who has lived a lie for so long, you happen to be very bad at it," Lucy crossed her arms and raised an eyebrow. "Now tell me the truth."

Lord Claybrook's head appeared from inside the library. He gazed at Elizabeth hanging on the door and then at Lucy. He opened his mouth and then quickly closed it.

"Have a nice day," he muttered, and before the girls could respond, sped away.

Elizabeth jumped down and glared at Lucy.

"You were trying to avoid him," Lucy put her hands up apologetically. "And instead of helping I sort of muddled it up."

"Precisely. I saw him walking towards the library, and I acted without thinking. I couldn't bear to face him, so I jumped and grabbed the top of the door and lifted my feet, hoping to avoid being seen. It worked. He never looked up and entered the library. I was about to slither down when you appeared and started demanding answers in that loud voice of yours."

"People say I am soft-spoken," Lucy said indignantly.

"Well, you are not," Elizabeth scowled.

"He is avoiding you just as much," Lucy said, linking her arm through Elizabeth's. "I saw him swallow a boiled egg this morning when you entered the dining room. He swallowed it whole, and before you had taken a step farther, he pushed his chair back and hurried away like a frightened walrus."

"He does not look like a walrus."

"He did a bit. I find that walruses look innocent, old and a bit guilty. He seemed to imbibe their spirit fairly well this morning."

"He is not old," Elizabeth objected.

Lucy steered her towards the gazebo, and they entered the shaded dome with a sigh. It had become their haven. A place where they knew they were alone, and no one was judging their every move.

The scent of rain, along with the heat of the gazebo, made them feel as if they had stepped into a different land. The thick vegetation climbing up walls and curling around marble statues looked greener than ever, and the cream and yellow jasmine flowers filled the air with a soft heady perfume.

Lucy's hair sprang up in protest and sweat began beading her forehead. She shed her parasol and coat and breathed a sigh of relief.

"I am sorry," she said, as soon as Elizabeth sat on the white wooden bench.

Elizabeth looked away.

Lucy crouched on the ground and peered up into Elizabeth's face. "I am sorry, for suspecting Lord Claybrook. I can't help it. I don't feel for him as you do, but I admit it was insensitive of me to say it."

Elizabeth bit her lip and ducked her head. "I feel nothing for him."

Lucy ignored that. "Here, my peace offering. My last bag of sugarplums and a slice of fruit cake."

Elizabeth stared at the squished cake and the sweets and laughed. "You are so childlike at times."

Lucy grinned. "Are we friends again?"

"I have to apologise too. I wasn't honest with you about my identity. I am sorry."

"Oh, I knew all about that. I was sitting outside the study window when you confessed it all to Lord Claybrook."

"And you never told me!"

"I was waiting for you to trust me enough to tell me yourself."

After a short silence, Elizabeth let out a sigh. "It's a difficult situation. So many lies and secrets. I have none left. You know it all now."

"Perhaps we can begin anew?" Lucy asked. She sprang up and dropped into a deep curtsy fit for a queen. "My name is Lucy Anne Trotter; I am a governess to the Willoughby children. And I stand accused of murder."

Elizabeth grinned and copied Lucy, "My name is Miss Elizabeth Verney, and I am a governess to the Claybrook children. And I, too, stand accused of murder."

"So much in common," Lucy giggled. "We should be friends."

"I would like that very much," Elizabeth replied, looking pleased.

"And I would like us to be friends for a long, long time. So, we must solve this crime quickly."

"I was wondering about the valet," Elizabeth said, sobering up.

"And I was wondering about the cook and the maids. I think we should focus on the servants next." Lucy popped a pineapple in her mouth and chewed furiously. "And you are right. The valet should be our first target."

Elizabeth nodded. "Let's dig out his secrets."

∞ ∞ ∞

Elizabeth

Elizabeth firmly tied the white bonnet string under her chin and hiked up her stockings. She had decided to follow the valet while Lucy had opted to search his room.

The valet, George Perris, was a mystery since he rarely indulged in gossip and kept to himself. He was like a handsome racehorse who made others feel like a lumbering cow in comparison. He was, perhaps, as old as her father, but from afar looked no older than Claybrook.

His clothes were always elegant, his movements graceful and his demeanour kind and welcoming. He seemed to be always smiling even though his mouth remained firm and straight, and the softness in his eyes gave him a dependable air.

She had watched the maids ogle him secretly, and she had to admit, the ease with which he carried Lord Aston would make any feminine heart tumble.

And yet, he rarely did anything to bring attention to himself and like a good servant, floated through the house like a wisp of smoke.

She glanced out the window and realised that he would be busy tending to Lord Aston's toilet. Perhaps, the servants could tell her a bit more about him?

She clutched the door leading to the hidden staircase and frowned. The servants would be guarded around her, but she would have to find a way to soften one of them up.

It would be a difficult task but not impossible. Squaring her shoulders, she headed to the kitchen.

"Cup of tea?" Elizabeth requested. She cleared her throat a few times before adding shrewdly, "My throat feels funny today."

The cook, who had three daughters of her own, thawed a bit. Her maternal instincts sprang up, and like a worried squirrel protecting her young, she got busy with the kettle. She added a few more bits of wood in the fire before sitting down at the table and handing Elizabeth a cup of chocolate.

"Better than tea," the cook muttered as she slid the cup across the table towards Elizabeth.

Elizabeth who hadn't had chocolate in weeks grasped the warm cup gratefully and took a sip. The chocolate slid down her throat warming her toes, and she sat back suddenly feeling chirpier and more confident.

"It's a cold day," Elizabeth began and coughed a tiny bit to keep up her act.

The cook melted further into the chair. Her eyes began to soften. "It is that."

"I wish Lord Aston would allow some heat in our rooms. It is difficult to sleep."

The cook nodded eagerly, the prospect of gossip enlivening her a little. "I always let my girls have warming pans on a cold night."

"You are kind," Elizabeth said. "I don't know how the servants have lived here for so many years. You would think with all the people poaching good servants, they would treat you right. The valet, for instance, seems so distinguished. He can easily get a better place to serve."

"Aye, the valet has been here the longest. I think it is loyalty that keeps him here. That and Lord Aston treats him better than anyone. Even his own sons, I suspect."

"Is he married?"

The cook nodded. "A wife, two sons and a baby girl. They live close by, and he goes home to them every evening. He is devoted to them. I have seen him reject the advances of many pretty maids over the years with my own eyes."

Elizabeth drained her chocolate, trying to think of more questions.

The cook rose and took the cup from her, "Hope you feel better soon, miss. I don't like seeing young ones ill."

Impulsively, Elizabeth kissed her cheek. "I wish you would trust me when I say I didn't kill anyone."

The cook patted her hand, her face flushed. "I trust no one," she responded gently.

Elizabeth left the kitchen feeling content and sleepy. The chocolate sat in her tummy like a warm, soft blanket, and she wished she could have sat by the kitchen fire and dozed off for a bit. But she had to find the valet, and for that, she needed to be alert.

She entered the dining room and found the servants bustling about. The scullery maid was poking one of the three fireplaces, coaxing the flames to burn higher. The maids were setting the table for breakfast, while the butler leaned against the doorway barking orders.

She swept by the scuttling servants and walked over to the window. The drapes had been pulled aside and she could see the beautiful woodland spread out in front of her. She marvelled at how close the majestic trees were to the house.

She opened the window and leaned as far out as she could. The fresh, cold air filled her lungs and woke her up from the spell the chocolate had put her in.

Her life had taken such an odd turn. She felt like a pot of soup that had been forgotten on the stove and boiled down to mere dregs. Dregs that were full of intense flavour, too potent for consumption.

Similarly, the events, emotions and feelings had become so intense in her life that she could barely stand it.

"Close the window," the scullery maid begged her.

She reluctantly did and went in search of the valet.

She found him quickly enough. He was hurrying towards Lord Aston's room. His face looked drawn, and he had dark smudges under his eyes.

Her eyebrows shot upwards when she spotted the crease in the back of his shirt and the scuff mark on his shoe.

She paused as soon as he slipped into Lord Astons' room.

After a moment's deliberation, she dropped to all fours and crawled the rest of the way to the door and peeked inside.

Lord Aston stood in front of his rocking chair while the valet was helping him undress. She closed one eye and watched in horror as the clothes fell to the floor. When the valet reached Lord Aston's unmentionables, she stifled a gasp and quickly shuffled backwards only to bump into a pair of magnificent legs.

Claybrook stared down at her, and she felt her entire body blush.

He held out his hand to her.

She stared at the long masculine fingers and bit her lip. A rush of feelings bubbled to the surface of her skin like a pot about to boil over. Her hand curled into a fist, and she ignored his hand and tried to stand on her own.

It was awkward getting up without help in her morning gown, but she managed it. Her face filled with triumph and she took a step back from him, the next moment her heel caught on her skirts, and she began flailing like a fish out of water.

He crossed his arms and watched her flap in amusement. This time he was not going to help her.

She waved her arms like a demented duck until she steadied herself and let out a sigh of relief.

"Women shouldn't crawl around on all fours," he said, with a twinkle in his eye. "And crash into men."

"Men shouldn't be so blind," she muttered back. "And no one crashed into anything. It was a bump."

"Women," he said, a little more loudly, "shouldn't be spying either."

"Men," she said, raising her own voice, "shouldn't blame women for murdering people if they think they are so delicate."

He scowled at her, and she frowned back at him.

It suddenly dawned on her that this was it. This was how she could face him without turning into a puddle of tears. All she had to do was argue with him every time she saw him. It was easier to be angry with him than deal with the awkwardness that had crept up between them since the kiss.

She tossed her head and stormed away. This strained, unnamed emotion between them was not her fault. She had not kissed him; *he* had kissed her. If anyone had the right to be indignant, it was her.

Back in her room, she found Lucy waiting for her.

"Anything?" Lucy asked.

Elizabeth nodded and filled her in.

"So, something is bothering the man. I wonder what?"

"Any clues in his room?"

"He keeps nothing," Lucy let out a frustrated sigh. "The man goes home every evening to his family, so all I found was a spare uniform, some shoe polish, sewing kit, soap, candles and some parchment and ink. Nothing useful. No letters, tokens or murder confessions."

"Why would he murder Beazley?" Elizabeth mused aloud.

"He could have been having an affair with Lady Willoughby," Lucy replied.

Elizabeth rolled her eyes. "Lady Willoughby couldn't be having an affair with so many men."

"Perhaps, he knew Beazley from before? Or, he could have been trying to kill Willoughby. Lord Willoughby used to fly into a temper and maltreat the servants. I know it is hard to believe now, what with him fearing his own shadow these days."

Elizabeth picked at a loose thread on her sleeve, "I can see the dignified valet objecting to having a shoe thrown at him."

"Precisely. It could be years of repressed anger that exploded one fine day."

"Hmm, who is next? The maids?"

"You tackle Mary while I will deal with Rosie," Lucy said, with a nod.

Chapter Twenty-Eight

Lucy

"Miss Trotter," Lord Adair called out.

"My lord, I was looking for Rosie," she said, dropping into a quick curtsy.

"Forget the maid and follow me."

"Where are we going?" she asked, bouncing after him.

He slowed down to allow her to keep up. "You will see."

He led her to the drawing-room.

The curtains had been pulled back, and sunlight streamed into the room, warm and golden. The blue-green tapestries on the wall rippled in the soft breeze that flew in from a partially open window. The pink leather sofa laden with soft gold and green cushions looked inviting for a change, but what drew her eye were the brown paper packages piled high on the sandalwood table near the fireplace.

"They are for you," he said, throwing aside the cushions lying on an armchair and sitting down.

"Eh?" she blinked in confusion.

"The packages are for you."

"For me?" she frowned. "Who sent them?"

"I bought some things for you, Miss Trotter."

He poured himself a cup of coffee. She noticed he turned it around three times before taking a sip. He was such an odd man with so many secrets and quirks. The more she watched him, the more she realised how complicated he was.

"Presents for me?" she eyed the packages suspiciously. "You are *bamming* me."

"I am doing no such thing," he said impatiently. "Open them, Miss Trotter, or I will be forced to do it for you. And I understand women find the act of opening presents just as thrilling as the gift within."

When she lingered uncertainly near the table, he reached over to the nearest parcel.

She snatched it out of his hands. "I will do it," she said, conceding defeat, and gingerly opening the first bag. "Sugared pineapples, mint cakes and sugared violets!"

Her face split into a wide smile and she popped a sweet into her mouth and sucked in delight. After that, he didn't have to encourage her. She pounced on the packages like a hungry monkey who has spotted a bunch of ripe bananas.

Shreds of brown paper and colourful strings flew into the air as she ripped open the parcels. A fine-looking fruit cake emerged from one bag, a peach, an orange and a nectarine rolled out of another, while the rest contained a bag of tea, a loaf of sweet bread, pastries, tins of coffee and biscuits."

"So much food," she said in awe.

"You look like you need fattening up. Too thin," Lord Adair commented.

She blushed. He had noticed her figure and her love for anything sweet.

"One more package left," he said, pointing to it.

He lit another cigar and finished his coffee.

She trotted over to the last bag and peered inside it. "It's a –

"Cape," he finished for her.

"A cape?" she squeaked, pulling out the soft green cloth and holding it to her face. "So soft, and it smells heavenly. But, I cannot accept this."

"Your clothes are ghastly. I cannot bear to look at them. Please, accept the cape and wear it every time I set my eyes on you. Your brown cardigan is hideous and that holey grey walking coat," he shuddered, "makes you look like an old-fashioned wig."

She caressed the cape, tears springing in her eyes, not because his words had offended her but because he had thought of her at all. She couldn't possibly accept the things . . . It was unseemly.

"I don't want you as my mistress," he said, guessing her thoughts. "I am simply helping a struggling orphan. It is an affliction. I cannot help it. I see a badly dressed woman, and I want to groom her, I see a skinny woman, and I want to feed her."

"I cannot accept charity. I have been pitied and lived off people's kindness all my life. I couldn't help it then, but I can do something about it now."

"Consider it a wage of sorts. You are trying to help me solve this crime. You are my eyes and ears in this place, and I pay all my informants handsomely."

"You are kind."

"I wish other women would see it as such. The last time I bought an apple for a young lady, she thought it was a proposal. I knew you would be more sensible."

Lucy dropped her lashes. It was true. She had fleetingly thought that maybe he wanted her, but the next moment, she had dismissed it as a ridiculous notion. She didn't think he would ever choose someone like her.

She looked up to find he was watching her keenly.

She popped a grape in her mouth and chewed nervously. "You bought me all of this to pay me for my work as an informant."

He nodded.

"Can you take it all away?"

"Why?"

"I want something else as payment."

His eyes narrowed.

She cleared her throat. "I wanted to ask if you could teach me how to land a facer."

"Eh?"

"I want to be a milling cove, I want to learn how to slash and parry with an Andrea Ferrara. I want to twist, leap and slice a man in two."

"Egad!"

"I want to brandish a barker, a spit and a snapper. I want to kick a flash man and save a lady's virtue, I want to juggle twenty knives, sniff out a goosecap and halloo."

"You are singing."

"Shall I go on."

He pressed his lips together. "Please smother the artist in you. I am becoming queasy."

She dipped her head and said shyly. "I am grateful for all the gifts but what I really want is . . . I want to learn how to fight. I don't want a man to save my bacon, I want to save my bacon. I want to learn how to throw a knife, use a hunga munga, and win at fisticuffs."

He smiled. "Most women ask me for protection, money, marriage, or...." He pursed his lips. "They want me to take care of them for the rest of their lives or find them a man who will, but you are asking me to teach you how to throw a knife?"

"The man I marry might die young; besides, no one can be around another person all the time. I need to know how to take care of myself and not depend on other people."

"You are refreshing, Miss Trotter."

"I want to learn how to take down a man, shoot him, kill him and bury him."

"You have conveyed your point most forcefully and at times even poetically. I am concerned with your bloodthirsty nature, Miss Trotter."

"I am not a squeamish young maid, my lord. I will make an excellent spy; seductive and ruthless."

He chuckled. "You are intriguing, artless and, mayhap, a bluestocking. Time will tell."

"So, will you help?"

"I will consider it if you agree to accept the presents."

She hesitated, "I can keep the food, the cape—"

"It is all or nothing, Miss Trotter."

She nodded, but in her heart, she promised herself that she

would pay him back one day.

She bit into a mint cake and chewed thoughtfully. He was warming to her presence. He had taken the time out to buy her things and patiently listened to her chatter.

True, he saw her more as a hungry, scruffy kitten that he had just procured and felt the need to groom and fatten up, but, she didn't mind. As long as he trained her to fight, and taught her some investigative skills, she was willing to do his bidding.

She watched him lean his head back on the cushion and make little rings of smoke with his cigar.

"Can you make hearts and such too?" she asked curiously.

He smiled. "Tell me about the valet," he asked instead and closed his eyes.

She began putting all the gifts in the bag, and while her hands worked, her mouth kept up a running commentary on all that they had found since they had spoken to him last.

When she finished, she found him fast asleep with the cigar dangling dangerously between his fingers.

She smiled at the sight. He looked so peaceful when he slept. She gently extracted the cigar and extinguished it, and then took her new green cape and covered as much of him as she could.

Finally, she threw a few more logs in the fireplace and left the room.

Chapter Twenty-Nine

Elizabeth

The girls were back in the gazebo, but this time, thunder and lightning danced in the sky like eager debutantes at a ball. The wind whizzed around like a conductor in an orchestra, and the rain slammed against the glass walls so hard that it felt as if the building would come crashing down around their quivering ears.

Elizabeth stared at the green cape draped around Lucy's shoulder and the blue veil covering the lower half of her face in confusion. "Why the veil and where did you procure it?"

Lucy smiled, or at least her eyes did since Elizabeth couldn't see her mouth. "I fashioned the veil out of one of the cushions in the parlor. No one will miss it. And as to why I am wearing it," she dropped her voice, "Last night, I was making my way back to my room after dinner, and I spotted a shadow following me. I tried catching the person, but he was too slippery. Therefore, I decided that I needed to disguise myself, so I am not followed again."

"I am sure plenty of people are following us," Elizabeth responded practically. "In fact, I think everyone is following everyone. And your disguise is awful."

"Fine, I wanted to look mysterious," Lucy conceded. "Dress the part and hope for an inspiration."

"You look ridiculous."

"I do not."

"Yes, you do."

"I think you are jealous of my veil."

"I will visit you in Bedlam once the rest of the world discovers your madness."

"No need to visit, you will have a bed next to mine." Lucy chuckled and blew a raspberry. "And before you ask, the cape is a gift from Lord Adair . . . a payment of sorts for helping him with this case."

Elizabeth glanced at the expensive fabric, worry creasing her brow. She was not helping him; he was helping *her*. He had come all the way to solve the crime and save her neck. Surely, she could see that. As for his kindness, it was bound to create windmills in her head.

"I know what you are thinking," Lucy said, grasping her hand. "I know he felt sorry for me and to save my pride, he said it was payment, not charity. And I know I am not even good enough to be his maid, forget his mistress. I see him as more of a benefactor, an angel if you will."

Elizabeth blushed. "I am sorry I was only concerned."

"I understand. I would have felt the same if our positions were reversed."

Elizabeth looked away. That was not true. Lucy had never questioned her feelings for Claybrook.

"Elizabeth? Are you well?"

She nodded and straightened her spine. "I spoke to Mary, and she said she was in the kitchen with the cook at the time of the murder. The cook did not deny it."

"But Mary was with the butler."

"Precisely. Which means, the cook has no alibi."

Lucy frowned. "The cook is on wobbly ground."

"Somehow, I don't think she did it," Elizabeth replied.

Lucy shrugged, "She could have detested Beazley while she worked for the family. Perhaps, he broke her daughter's heart . . . or her own? On the morning of the murder, the cook could have been standing at the kitchen window and spotted him walking towards the forest."

"In a trice, her past would have risen in her mind like a wounded beast, and she would have reached for the gin and taken a swig. Then blind with years of suppressed anger, she could have raced after him. Once they were deep into the forest, she would have produced a blunderbuss and

BANG!"

"She would have fired the gun and shot the man dead."

Elizabeth gulped, "Now, I am scared of the cook."

"She probably didn't kill him."

"We can't be certain."

Lucy sighed. "Is anything certain in life?"

Elizabeth watched the rivulets of water on the windowpanes trickle down and mix with the earth. She recalled her childhood dreams and the carefree way she had lived. She remembered how she and her sisters used to run in the fields picking thistles and daisies and bringing them home for her mother. She had noticed her mother's smile but not the deepening lines on her forehead.

She looked at Lucy unhappily. "If only we could be little girls again."

"I wouldn't like that," Lucy shrugged. "I wouldn't want to go back to being hungry and trapped and watch my friends die every year."

Elizabeth's mouth turned down. She was once again reminded how much harder Lucy's life had been, but looking at her now, so full of life and humour, it was easy to forget.

Lucy suddenly clapped her hands and did a little twirl. "I have a great idea."

"What?"

"Let's get the cook drunk."

"Big fleas have little fleas upon their backs to bite them, and little fleas have lesser fleas, and so ad infinitum."

"Eh?"

"You were doling out bags of moonshine, so I decided to do the same."

"It's not moonshine. If we get her foxed, she might confess all she knows about the maids. She might even confess to the murder."

"It will never work. What an absurd idea."

Lucy folded her arms across her chest and glared at her. "So, are we getting the cook drunk or not?"

Elizabeth sighed. "Since I can think of nothing better . . . fine."

Lucy grinned. "When?"

"Tonight? But where will we get the gin?"

"I will ask Lord Adair for some. He is bound to have something of the sort."

"Aren't you afraid to ask him?"

Lucy nodded enthusiastically. "Terrified. But that never stopped me."

Chapter Thirty

Lucy

"I got brandy, Liz," Lucy said, bursting into Elizabeth's room.

"Brandy? Show me." Elizabeth replied sceptically.

Lucy dipped her hand into the hidden slit in her skirt and pulled out a small bottle filled with what looked like liquid honey. "Lord Adair does not go near gin."

"I didn't think he would." She uncorked the bottle and sniffed the contents. "Mmm, perhaps, we should save this for ourselves."

"Elizabeth?"

"Yes?"

"If the fumes of the brandy have meddled with your head then I wonder what taking a sip would do?"

"Should I try?"

"I am curious, I admit, to see the effect, but we need to focus on the plan."

"I want to take a sip."

"Instead, pray to Dionysus to lift this fog of madness," Lucy responded and snatched the bottle back. "Come along now, my higgeldy piggeldy friend, we need to catch the cook before she goes to bed."

"Fine," she reluctantly agreed. "But, I still think this is a terrible idea. That gorgeous brandy is going to go to waste."

They grabbed a shawl each and headed out of the room.

The hallway was dark and cold; they gripped each other's hands and stayed close. Suddenly, being stealthy and their aim of getting the cook drunk struck them both as hilarious.

They began giggling and snorting like little piglets, which made the whole thing even more ridiculous. Soon they were biting their hands in an attempt to stifle their laughter.

They turned a corner, and their smiles died like they had been bashed over the head with a mallet.

Claybrook stood in front of them wearing a fake moustache, a black beard and a top hat.

Elizabeth stared at him.

Claybrook stared at her.

The grandfather clock ticked away in the background while Lucy side-eyed the two of them.

Elizabeth and Claybrook continued staring at each other as if a fascinating play were being enacted in each other's eyeballs.

Lucy cleared her throat loudly, coughed, hacked and gripped her throat and thrashed about.

It didn't work.

Elizabeth and Claybrook remained still as rocks, their eyes glued to each other as if joined by an invisible string.

"The rabbits are smoking cigars and elephants are laying eggs," Lucy snapped.

Elizabeth blinked first and stared at Lucy. "W- what did you say?"

"It's a nice evening."

"It's raining," Claybrook remarked, finally emerging from the spell that had momentarily struck him speechless.

"I happen to like rain," Lucy replied, her eyes big and wide and full of meaning as she stared at Elizabeth.

"We were going to get a glass of milk," Elizabeth said, catching her drift.

"Cook will have some," Lucy nodded quickly.

Claybrook stood aside, his broad, muscular figure not giving much room for the girls to move past without brushing him.

Elizabeth went first. She turned beet red by the time she took the two necessary steps to cross him.

"Nice moustache," Lucy grinned, when it was her turn to whizz. "Where are you off to?"

"I am heading to the butchers to get a pound of mutton," he responded straight-faced. "Just like you are heading to the kitchens to get some milk from the cook."

Lucy winked at him, leaving him spluttering in shock and dragged Elizabeth away.

"How are we going to get the cook drunk?" Lucy muttered outside the kitchen.

"Leave it to me," Elizabeth replied confidently. She seemed to have recovered from her encounter with Claybrook.

Lucy hoped she never turned into a blithering lovestruck fool like her. It was revolting.

"How are you feeling," the cook asked, the moment she saw Elizabeth.

"Not well," she sighed, the lingering blush on her cheek gave her words an air of authenticity.

Lucy clasped her hands in front of herself and widened her eyes. "Can I warm some milk for her?"

The cook threw her rag down and nodded, "I will put some on."

"Lord Adair gave me a bit of brandy," Elizabeth said weakly. "He thought it would help."

Lucy produced the bottle on cue. "I could add a drop in her milk."

The cook eyed the brandy thirstily.

"He said I could have the entire bottle. Such a generous man," Lucy continued.

"I am no drunk," Elizabeth objected. "A drop is plenty. Although, I feel a bit bold drinking on my own. Maybe you can join me? A drop of brandy in your tea will do you no harm."

The cook needed no further prompting. The teacups appeared on the table along with a steaming pot of tea in no time.

Lucy added a generous splash in the cook's tea and Elizabeth's milk. She decided to avoid the temptation and keep a clear head.

It took four cups of tea laced with brandy for the cook to lean back in her seat and relax.

Lucy and Elizabeth spent some time asking her all about her daughters and the cook thawed even more.

Soon the cook was leaning back comfortably, her arm draped over the adjoining seat and her feet up on the chair across from her. Her eyes were beginning to glaze, and her mouth had relaxed into a demented smile.

The clock struck midnight, and the house went quiet and dark.

Lucy glanced at the dying embers in the fireplace and proceeded to light a small candle.

The click, click of the tinder box filled the room, and soon, the little flame created eerie shadows on the walls.

The cook's round face was flushed red, and her dark eyes looked like lamplights. She didn't look so kind and jovial anymore, but somewhat sinister and Lucy exchanged a nervous glance with Elizabeth.

Elizabeth took a deep breath and spoke in a light, measured tone. "Did you know Rosie was with Lady Willoughby when the murder took place."

"They could have done it together," the cook said, taking a big gulp of the tea.

"Lady Willoughby seems mighty fond of Rosie," Lucy prompted.

The cook nodded. "That girl may have a pinched face, but she knows her job and better yet, knows how to hold on to secrets."

Lucy leaned forward. "But why would Rosie kill Beazley?"

"No reason," the cook shrugged. "But if the target was Lord Willoughby, then she had plenty of reason. Loyalty towards her missus may have prompted her to do so, or her ladyship asked her to."

Elizabeth frowned. "And Mary? What reason could she have for killing Beazley or Lord Willoughby?"

"I don't think she could have done it. If Lord Willoughby died, then nothing would keep the butler away from Lady Willoughby. And Mary is gone on the butler. I have seen her mooning after 'im often enough."

"Where was she during the time of the murder?" Lucy wondered, splashing more brandy into the cook's cup.

The cook sipped and said, "She was with the butler. I heard them in the larder."

Lucy and Elizabeth exchanged a glance.

"What do you think of Lord Willoughby? Why would anyone want to kill him?" Lucy asked.

"Not a nice man," the cook slurred. "Jealous of his brother. Lord Aston always favoured his younger son and understandably so. Lord Willoughby paws the maids, whines and whinges, has more airs than a lady. And he gets something furious when he gambles. Curses like a sailor, throws cups and plates around. No, not a nice man at all."

"And Beazley . . . I wonder if he had any enemies," Elizabeth said carefully.

"No. Beazley was a bit of lamb. His wife, now, is awful . . . a real harridan but him . . . he wouldn't hurt a fly. A sweet man," the cook said fondly. "Sad, he died the way he did. He deserved better."

"I heard he chased skirts as well," Lucy said.

The cook shrugged, "Which man doesn't?"

"Claybrook," Elizabeth spoke up. "I have never seen him paw anyone."

"He is a rare one," the cook agreed. "But you can't blame Beazley for doing what most men do. The maids understand. That's how things are."

Elizabeth and Lucy exchanged another glance.

When they turned back, the cook was asleep, her head lolling to the side.

Lucy folded her shawl and placed it on the table and then gently laid the cook's head on top of it. Elizabeth threw her own brown cardigan around the cook's shoulder, and the two girls tiptoed out of the room.

"The cook didn't kill him," Lucy remarked, the moment they were back in her room.

"She heard the butler and Mary in the larder, and she couldn't have if she were busy traipsing through the forest." Elizabeth agreed.

"Plus, she seemed fond of Beazley."

"Rosie seems to be in the clear too," Elizabeth said.

"Rosie has a motive … but is she capable of that much love for Lady Willoughby that she would agree to kill a man for her?"

"I doubt it. The woman does everything for selfish reasons. I don't see her putting her neck on the noose even for her own children."

"We are finally getting somewhere," Lucy yawned.

"We need to dig deeper into the family," Elizabeth said thoughtfully.

"You can find out about Claybrook," Lucy nudged her and grinned. "We need more information, and he is bound to spill something with your beautiful eyes staring at him."

"Oh hush," she blushed.

"You have to, Liz," Lucy said, sobering up. "You have to use what weapons you have. We need answers. Time is running out."

Elizabeth gulped and nodded. "I will try."

Chapter Thirty-one

Lucy

It was the egg that did it.

Lucy watched Lady Willoughby fling the egg across the breakfast table. It slammed against the wall leaving a grey and yellow smear.

She felt a little guilty. She knew why the breakfast was less than pleasant this morning. She had gotten the cook drunk, and the subsequent effects were showing in the hasty breakfast thrown on the table this morning.

The cook was summoned. She staggered into the room and bumped into the back of the sofa. Her eyes were veiny and bloodshot, and her curly white hair was standing tall and springy on one side of her head while the other was smeared with flour and stuck to her scalp in unsightly clumps.

She blinked questioningly at Lady Willoughby.

"The egg," Lady Willoughby raged, "was cold as ice."

The cook frowned. "It was warm when I sent it up."

"I like my eggs hot," she retorted. "This was cold. Are you calling me a liar?"

"I," the cook swayed in confusion as if words were taking a few moments to penetrate the brandy fog enveloping her head.

The lack of immediate apology incensed Lady Willoughby even more. All of cook's past mistakes sprang forth in her mind, and she shot them out like an overexcited blunderbuss.

"You, incompetent fool," she raged. "You were late sending the breakfast up this morning, the beef during the dinner party was tough as a shoe, you are constantly unwell, you make the same boring things over and over again for us to eat, you go on and on about your daughters like they are royalty, you gossip like a fish wife, and you haven't even bothered to look presentable before coming up to see me!"

The cook gasped and staggered back. Her hand flew to her mouth, and the other clutched the apron around her belly.

Lady Willoughby narrowed her eyes and said the inevitable. "I wonder who recommended you. I must write to them and complain."

The cook began swaying like a church bell on Sunday.

Lady Willoughby, oblivious to the teetering cook, began rummaging through the contents of her brain. Her eyes widened, and she sprang to her feet in shock. "Beazley recommended you. How could I have forgotten? You worked for his family for years before coming to us!"

The cook paled, the fog lifted, and panic descended. The terror was evident on her face. "I didn't kill him," she croaked. "I swear it. I only stopped working for them since my youngest got married to the lamplighter who lives in this town and I wanted to live close to her. London was too expensive for the likes of us, and Lord Beazley very kindly understood and found me a position here—"

"Stop your blithering," Lady Willoughby snapped, reaching for the bell. She rang it furiously until the butler appeared. "Tell everyone to assemble in the morning room at once. I have found the murderer."

The butler's eyes widened, and his mouth opened to ask questions when he realised Lord Willoughby and Claybrook were present in the room as well as Lucy. So, he bowed and hurried away.

Once everyone including Lord Aston, Lord Adair and the servants had arrived, Lady Willoughby clapped her hands. "Silence, I have an important piece of information to impart. I had completely forgotten about it, until this morning, when I was sent a ghastly egg to eat for breakfast. It was not only cold but overcooked and grey."

"The state of your breakfast eggs is of no concern of mine," Lord Aston snapped.

"This is not about the eggs," Lady Willoughby retorted.

"Then get on with it and no need to digress. I don't want to know how insipid your coffee was or how maudlin your toast," Lord Aston muttered impatiently.

Lady Willoughby pinched her lips and walked towards the top of the room. Once there, she turned dramatically to face them all.

This was her moment, and she was going to take her time to shine as bright as possible and for as long as she could.

"Hurry up, woman," Lord Aston growled, throwing a log into the fire and loosening his shirt.

Lady Willoughby ignored him, "A few years ago, our cook ran away. It turned out he had been a pirate, and the lure of the sea had been too much for him. Hence, I started looking for a new cook."

Lord Aston threw another log in the fire and took off his breeches.

Lady Willoughby hurried on, "As you know, servants are hard to come by, and after an entire month of searching Lord Willoughby ran into someone who had a cook at his London lodgings wanting to leave his employ and move to the country. She came with a great reference, and we hired her immediately. Can you guess who that person was and who recommended her?"

"I didn't kill him," the cook burst out.

"Anyone? Can you guess?" Lady Willoughby smiled like a smug cat.

Lord Adair threw his cigar into the ashtray and offered a bored shrug. "Simply because Beazley recommended the cook, does not mean she killed him. In fact, it would be foolish on the cook's part to continue living in this house knowing that she was the only one with any past connection with him. Perhaps, she felt that since she was innocent, she didn't need to run."

"But she could have done it!" Lady Willoughby snapped.

"She could have," Lord Adair acceded her point. "But then so could you."

"She loves her daughter too much," Lucy spoke up. "Had she run, her daughters would have had to suffer for her deeds."

Lord Claybrook leaned forward in his chair. "Since Beazley had recommended her, it would appear, he or at least his wife, had been fond of her, and she did not leave their employ in disgrace. I agree with Adair. Simply because the cook knew him from before, does not mean she killed him. We need more evidence."

"You will no longer work here, cook," Lady Willoughby's wounded ego cried. "I don't care what anyone thinks. I know you did it."

"This morning you were convinced the governesses did it," Lord Claybrook commented.

"They all did it," she retorted childishly.

"I am afraid the cook will have to remain here until the case is solved," Lord Aston grinned. "But now that she no longer works for you, my dear, who will make tonight's dinner? I would like some onion soup, cheese wigs, stewed calf ears and gooseberry fool."

Lady Willoughby turned apoplectic, and a slew of fascinating expressions crossed her face as pride warred with laziness in her heaving bosom. She finally glared at the cook. "You may continue your duties until I have found your replacement."

"She will poison us all," Lord Willoughby howled from a dark shadow in the corner.

"Then you cook the deuced meals," Lady Willoughby snapped.

Lucy slipped out of the room, feeling relieved that Lord Adair had prevented the family from making hasty decisions yet again.

In a way, she had been responsible for the disclosure of the cook's past. After all, she had gotten the cook drunk; hence, the cook had made a horrible breakfast and vexed Lady Willoughby.

She reached her room and sat down at her desk. At least, the butler could no longer blackmail the cook. She picked up the love letter letters she had found in his room and slammed them on the table, wishing it was his head.

How could she have thought the man was handsome? All she saw now was an oily, despicable creature who enjoyed preying on helpless women.

That slubber de gullion, beau nasty deserved to sit on a porcupine saddle for the rest of his life.

She pulled out a roll of cheap parchment and dipped her pen in ink. After a moment's thought, she began writing to the girls explaining all about butler's nature and his blackmailing tactics. She attached the letter they had sent to him, so he would have no means to extract money from them in the future.

She knew some girls wouldn't believe her, but some might. Even if one girl out of the fifteen who had written to him, took her seriously, then she would feel like she had accomplished something.

Posting so many letters would be dear. She didn't know how she would manage it. She fingered the green silk cape and wondered if she could sell it.

She was signing the last letter off with an assumed name when Lord Adair walked in.

Immediately the room seemed to shrink to half its size. She leapt up, embarrassed at her own dishevelled state and the state of the room.

She smoothed her hair and skirt and took a staggering step forward.

He wrinkled his nose at her petticoat lying on the floor and wet stockings dangling on the back of her chair.

She snatched the stockings and shoved it into her petticoat pocket.

"What were you doing?" he asked, frowning at the pile of letters on her desk.

She told him, and his eyes softened. "Good girl," he said, and for a moment she felt like he was going to reach out and pat her head like she was an adorable Pekingese.

She stuck her tongue between the gap in her teeth and waited for him to say more.

"Do you need anything?" he asked, looking around her room.

She shook her head.

"Some ink?"

"Oh no, thank you," she lied. He had done enough. She didn't want him to feel sorry for her and treat her like an orphan again.

He frowned but nodded, respecting her wishes.

"Is that all?" she asked.

"I will post those for you," he said, reaching for the pile of letters.

"I have a . . . question," she said carefully.

"You want to work for me."

Her mouth dropped open.

"And," he added with a twinkle in his eyes, "You want to do that because you want to find your parents with the new skills you will learn as a spy."

Her eyes widened in shock. No wonder people thought Lord Adair had extraordinary powers.

"I can't read your mind," he said, responding to her unspoken question. "But I know you."

She bit her lip, "Will you teach me?"

He stood for a moment looking at her face and then without a word turned on his heels and left the room.

She blinked after him, feeling confused. Did he not respond because he didn't want to hurt her feelings, or was he considering it? And why had he come to her room in the first place?

Chapter Thirty-Two

Elizabeth

Elizabeth sat on the hard bed in her room and wondered how to question Claybrook. She had tried it before and failed miserably.

"Pull your bodice down a bit," Lucy bounded into the room.

Elizabeth blinked in confusion. "Eh?"

Lucy tutted impatiently. "Here," she said, adjusting Elizabeth's green gown, so the tops of her bosom showed a bit more.

Elizabeth crossed her arms over her chest. "I am not going out like this."

Lucy placed her hands on her hips. "Don't you recall that girl who came for the party pretending to be rained upon when it hadn't rained in two whole days? Compared to her, you are barely showing anything."

"This is indecent."

"Is not," Lucy said, fussing with Elizabeth's hair.

She stared at the cracked mirror on the wall. "I look dishevelled. You have pulled half my hair out of the bun."

Lucy smiled. "You look beautiful. The loose strands are framing your face beautifully."

"I shall not leave the room looking like this."

Lucy shrugged. "Please yourself. When we are walking towards the noose, you can feel proud that you retained your modesty, if not your neck. When you are a skeleton in the grave, you can crow over the fact that you never let a man set eyes on your secret charms. When you are a ghost, you can lecture other ghosts on propriety and good manners. Then you can be the Grande dame of all ghosts and conduct dances in haunted castles."

"Oh, alright, I will try. But he barely answered my questions the last time. I doubt my tangled hair will enchant him into baring his soul."

"Don't ask him anything. Talk about yourself. Become a little maudlin, a little helpless, and he will unfurl like a rose on a summer's day."

"Where did you learn to be so manipulative?"

"We had to learn every trick to get what we wanted in the orphanage. I learned to stay invisible, keep my ears open and deal with all sorts of people."

Elizabeth raised her brow.

"I didn't say I was any good at it. I *know* what to do, but I somehow fail in the end. Anyhow, you are a natural. Look at the way you have the cook twisted around your finger. Even Lady Willoughby liked you at one point. You do it so effortlessly and beautifully."

Elizabeth softened at the compliment. "I will try."

A few hours later, Elizabeth sat in the library feeling vexed. How had Lucy convinced her to speak to Claybrook, that, too, while looking like she had forgotten to comb her hair?

She pulled her bodice up and ran her fingers through her tresses in irritation. The bun had fallen apart soon after she had left the room.

Thereafter, she had spent a while searching for Claybrook to quiz him. Every time she spotted the blasted man and tried to follow him, he vanished like a magician.

She lay her head on the book in front of her. It was a beautiful green and gold book that had painted illustrations of the royal family. Most of the pictures depicted the regent and his wife in humorous situations, but they failed to bring a smile on her face.

Instead, the smell of books and ink reminded her of her father and she suddenly ached to see him one more time. She had loved him dearly, and she knew he had loved her best amongst all her sisters.

She wished she could kiss his weathered cheek and lay her head on his chest. She wished she could hear him speak one more time and tell her that everything would be alright.

"I wish you were alive," she sighed softly.

"Who are you thinking of?"

She jerked her neck in the direction of the voice and found Claybrook leaning against the doorway. How long had he been watching her?

"Ouch," she yelped, as a moment later, pain shot through her neck.

"That sudden twist must have pulled a muscle," he said, coming up to her. "Is it bad?"

"Nothing I can't bear," she said, gripping her neck and trying not to cry out again.

He gently took her fingers away and placed his own warm hand on her neck.

She squirmed under his touch.

"Stay still, a moment," he urged as his thumb began massaging the taut muscle.

"What were you thinking about?" he asked as his hand moved from her neck to her shoulder.

"Hmm?"

"Elizabeth?"

She stood up and took a step away from him. "What did you say?"

He watched her take another step back.

She frowned. "Why are you s-smiling?"

"What were you thinking about?"

"Home . . . my father . . . death."

"Death?"

"Not long, now, before I am blamed for the murder," she whispered. "Death is inevitable. I find myself thinking of it often."

"Did you love your father very much?"

"More than anything."

"And your sisters?"

"I love them too. You wouldn't think it if you saw us together."

He leaned his hip against the table. "I don't approve of my brother much. His conduct is unbecoming of our family name. He is on a path to ruin, and if it continues, his children will be left destitute."

"Your aunt must have loved you very much since she bestowed her wealth and title on you. Was she childless?"

"She had one daughter who could not inherit. I took care of her until she married a wealthy man. She is happy, and that's all my aunt asked of me. She wanted me to ascertain that her precious child was happy and taken care off."

"Happiness," she mused softly, "such a simple thing and yet so hard to come by."

They stood in silence for a bit, each lost in thought.

After a moment, he asked, "Did you kill him, Miss Verney?"

"No," she replied tremulously. "That's what makes this harder. These accusations have created a cloud of terror that haunt me constantly. I made a mistake and hid my identity, but I did not kill anyone."

"I understand."

"Do you believe me?"

"I want to."

Her heart leapt, and she reached out and caught his hand. Her eyes were luminous and beseeching when she spoke. "Did you kill him? I heard you arguing with Beazley after you saved me that day. I had followed you . . . I overheard you threatening to kill him if he so much as looked at the women in this house. And the next morning he was dead."

"You didn't tell anyone," he said, knowing it for a fact.

She dipped her head to hide her face. She didn't know what to say.

He caught her chin and forced her to look up. "Why didn't you tell anyone, Elizabeth?"

"No one would have believed me."

"You didn't even admit it to Miss Trotter. Surely, she would have believed you."

"How do you know?"

"She would have confessed it to Adair. She wouldn't keep a thing like that a secret, not from Adair."

"Does he know?"

"I told him."

She gasped. "But that means—"

"I am a suspect as much as you are."

"But you are innocent."

"How can you be certain?"

"I just am."

"Such faith. It's touching."

She blushed, wondering if he was mocking her.

His knuckles caressed her pink cheeks. "I should be contemplating death, as well. After all, I could be convicted—"

Her fingers shot to his lips, and her eyes filled with horror. "Do not say it. They wouldn't hang you. Why, you are titled. You could escape to France... or India. No one would find you and with all your wealth—"

He cupped her face and stared down at her. "Calm yourself."

"I am calm," she cried. "I just think you should be on a boat to someplace safe. I could pack you lunch; perhaps, you can take some gold. Your previous cook was a pirate, mayhap, he can help spirit you away—"

"Hush. Nothing will happen to me, nor will I let anything happen to you, not while I live."

She froze at his words and the unspoken meaning behind them.

He dipped his head and kissed her slowly. "You look enchanting tonight," he said, roughly.

Footsteps in the corridor had them spring apart.

She stared at him while her hand flew to her mouth in shock. What was wrong with them? They shouldn't be touching, let alone kissing. He was titled, and she was a lying, cheating village girl.

And yet, the way he was looking at her now, she felt . . . treasured.

Oh, he was muddling her brain!

Sometimes, she thought he hated her for deceiving him, and yet he had kept her lies a secret. He had protected her and raged at her when she had confessed to the family that she was not Jane, but Elizabeth.

And now, these intimate moments . . . what was she to make of them? Why did he care what happened to her? Why had he kissed her again?

He could never marry her; she would never be his mistress.

"Elizabeth?"

She dipped under his arm and fled. One more kiss and she would have invited him to her bed.

Chapter Thirty-Three

Lucy

"I hate silent nurseries." Lucy dragged a small chair towards the children's desk and sat down.

Elizabeth joined her. "Master Willoughby has been sent away because of the pudding incident; hence, this is the best place to discuss our next plan. It's far more secluded than our rooms."

Lucy eyed the cold fireplace, the thick dusty drapes and the toys quietly lined up in the corner. "I think he was glad to go."

Elizabeth lay a comforting hand on Lucy's arm, "He was becoming lonely. It's for the best."

Lucy nodded. "Everyone has been having the fit of the blue devils, and it was beginning to affect him too."

"Shall we discuss all we have learnt so far?" Elizabeth asked, changing the topic.

"Yes, please," Lucy replied gratefully. If she became any gloomier, she would begin to wail, beat her chest and thrash about.

Elizabeth pulled out a piece of cheap parchment from her reticule while Lucy arranged the pen, ink and sand for dusting on the table.

"List of Suspects," Lucy began scribbling.

"Lord Willoughby," Elizabeth said immediately. "He said he was in a bathtub. Therefore, he has no alibi and a strong motive.

He could have lost money while gambling with Beazley and didn't want to pay him. Beazley could have found out about the butler and his wife having an affair and tried to blackmail him."

Lucy wrote it all down and added, "He knew Beazley best, and he could have been nursing a grudge against him for years. I can think of innumerable other reasons."

"Next, Lady Willoughby was with her maid Rosie," Elizabeth said, "but, I doubt Rosie loves her ladyship enough to kill."

"Unless she has been showered with *bobs* and *beans*." Lucy popped a lemon drop in her mouth and sucked thoughtfully. "A precious ring, a string of pearls, pounds to help her buy her own home and live a comfortable life. We can't rule her out. Nor can we rule out Lady Willoughby or that horrendous butler."

"Lord Claybrook," Elizabeth's voice caught on his name.

Lucy chose to remain silent.

Elizabeth cleared her throat. "He said he didn't do it. I spoke to him l-last evening, and I believe him."

Lucy watched her blush. "And?"

"He said he wasn't fond of his brother, since he was squandering all the money, but he didn't kill him."

"Did he kiss you?"

"Lucy!"

She grinned, "He did! I can see it on your face. How was it?"

"The valet," Elizabeth quickly wrote down.

"Did you swoon?"

"Where was the valet?"

"Did Claybrook tickle your chin? Did he call you darling, dumpling and num nums?"

"Stop it, or I will bash your head with the fire poker."

Lucy sighed dramatically. "Fine, let's get back to the deuced murder. The valet was with Lord Aston."

"He could have a hidden motive."

"I suppose."

"Lord Aston?" Lucy rolled the sweet around on her tongue. "What do we know about him?"

"He is a bit mad."

"He married the king's favourite aunt, that's how he was bestowed his title."

"I heard he went dotty after his wife died."

"He seems sharp enough to me," Lucy argued.

"Perhaps."

Lucy drummed her fingers on the table. "He can barely walk a few steps before needing the valet's assistance. He refuses to use the sedan chair, though, at times, he has no choice."

Elizabeth leaned back in her chair and stretched. "He has a lot of pride."

"Would he kill Beazley though?"

"Could he," Elizabeth countered.

"He is not feigning his ill health," Lucy replied thoughtfully. "That I am certain of."

"Then it would have been difficult."

"The cook, the butler and Mary couldn't have done it," Lucy said. "The cook overheard the butler and Mary in the larder. So that proves that the three of them were in the house."

"Unless the cook overheard them discussing their little romance later in the day and used that information to prove her innocence."

Lucy slammed her head on an old history book lying on the desk. "Everyone is a suspect."

Elizabeth sighed. "So, all this while, our efforts have been for not."

The door flew open. "Girls, pack your bags."

Elizabeth and Lucy shot to their feet.

Lady Willoughby stood before them wearing a long, green, and red silk robe with gold embroidery and black satin slippers. Her blonde hair fell straight and stiff around her pink face, while her sparkling eyes attached themselves to Elizabeth.

"Why do we have to pack?" Lucy asked.

"Did I tell you the Duke of Firth is a great admirer of mine?" Lady Willoughby purred. "He had even stayed with us once. An extremely handsome man."

"What's that got to do with us leaving?" Elizabeth snapped.

Lucy turned away and opened the window, feeling sick. A strong east wind rushed in, making her shiver. She guessed what Lady Willoughby was going to say.

Lady Willoughby's smile broadened as she spoke. "I wrote to the Duke and told him that I needed his help to solve a crime committed in his dukedom. In fact, he should have been the one solving it in the first place."

"Lord Adair is famed for his skills as an investigator," Lucy said, turning back to face her.

"Are you doubting the Duke's capabilities, my dear?

"Are you doubting Adair's?" Lucy shot back.

"It's the Duke's prerogative to decide who should handle a murder committed on his land. I simply offered him some well-meaning advice."

"What do you mean?" Elizabeth asked.

Lady Willoughby shot her a look of loathing. "I told him everything. All about the murder, and my suspicions regarding a certain governess and her friend. How one of the girls had assumed the name of a dead lady, while the other had been part of a murder investigation previously. And he agreed with my conclusion."

Elizabeth paled. "What conclusion?"

Lady Willoughby rolled her eyes. "Do I need to spell everything out? He wrote back saying he will be here by tomorrow evening. He is coming here to arrest you both for murdering Lord Beazley. Isn't that wonderful?"

"How could you?" Lucy growled.

"He is mine," Lady Willoughby responded, her voice tremulous. "I have waited for him for years. As soon as the real killer takes care of my husband, I will be free to marry him."

"The butler?"

"The butler!" she responded, shocked. "I can't marry a butler. He will remain in my employ and be well compensated for his services. I have loved only one man in my life, and that's Claybrook. I will not let an upstart take my place by his side."

"But you thought the cook was to blame."

"I still think it's her, but, then I decided that getting rid of you two is far more important than sending a fairly decent cook to the gallows."

"You are making a dreadful mistake," Elizabeth cried.

"You shouldn't have kissed him," she shot back, her eyes wild with hatred. "I saw you in the library."

Elizabeth grasped Lucy's hand. "We need to speak to Lord Adair."

Lucy eyed Lady Willoughby standing in the doorway with her long, golden hair tangling in the breeze and her red and green silk robe swirling around her like a loony bat.

She bowed her head and admitted defeat. "We need his help. We have run out of time."

∞∞∞

Lucy found Lord Adair standing near a small artificial pond behind the house. He was leaning on his cane, lost in thought.

She dawdled near an ancient oak, wondering what to say to him. The east wind had not let up, and she adjusted her cape, glad of its warmth. A sudden poignant feeling shot through her as she realised that Lord Adair, who saw her as a nuisance at best, was the closest thing she had to family.

Ever since she had left the orphanage and started her new life six months ago, he had been the only constant. He had come to her aid, again and again, perhaps because he felt sorry for her.

She knew she was just one of the many people in England dependent on him, and he saw her as a pet that he remembered now and then when she yelped.

But for her, he was her anchor. His presence gave her the strength to fight and dream of a respectable life. He gave her hope that if things went dreadfully wrong, he would right them.

She was not in love with him, but what she felt when she looked at him was . . . admiration, respect, fondness, and concern. His life was always in danger and if anything happened to him . . . her heart stopped even thinking about it.

Did he realise how important he was to her?

"Miss Trotter, stop daydreaming and come here."

Lucy stared at his back in surprise. "How did you know it was me?"

"I just did."

She went and stood by his side and mimicked his pose. The water was shimmering green and gold in the sunlight, a few thistles and dandelions wrestled in the breeze farther afield.

It was cold, but it was spring with the promise of summer on the breeze.

She watched the delicate blades of grass, and the fragile shoots dig in their heels and stay put, while the wind tried to rip them apart.

She crossed her arms as a burst of energy rushed through her. She couldn't give up now that she was so close. She had to prove herself to Adair. Otherwise, her future looked bleak; She would live an ordinary life working in a dreary job, marry a farmer, bear a few children, and go to her grave full of questions.

Her hair escaped its pins and whipped around her head in abandon.

Ordinary. The word irked her.

She tucked a strand behind her ears and turned to face him. "One hint. No more."

He glanced at her. "Ah, so you think I have solved it."

"Haven't you?"

"You know me well."

She shook her head. "No one can understand you, my lord, but I believe in you."

He looked away. "Do you want me to end it all?"

"Not yet. One hint and one day. Please, that's all I ask. The duke will be here tomorrow, and I will know who killed Beazley before then, I swear it. I will find him out."

"The murderer didn't care who he killed. He wanted both the men dead."

"What?"

"The target was both the men, Miss Trotter, and that's your hint."

Chapter Thirty-Four

Lucy

Lucy went in search of Elizabeth and found her hiding under the piano in the music room.

"Claybrook?" Lucy asked, sitting down on a dusty sofa. Elizabeth nodded. "Was he outside?"

"No, you can come out now."

Elizabeth slithered out and sheepishly joined her.

"I spoke to Lord Adair and—"

"And?" Elizabeth prompted.

She took out a piece of fruit cake and started picking raisins from it. "I need to tell you something before that."

Elizabeth frowned. "What's the matter?"

"I wanted to investigate the murder, not because I didn't think Lord Adair would do a fair job and find the killer, but because I wanted to prove to him that I could solve this crime as well. I had been successful once, surely, I could do it again and convince him that I would be an asset and he could use me as his assistant."

"You want to be a detective?" Elizabeth laughed. "But that's madness. You are a woman, Lucy."

"I wanted to learn investigative skills and then discover what happened to my parents."

"Oh."

"I can't fail now. Not after coming this far."

"Does Lord Adair know who murdered Beazely?" Elizabeth asked.

Lucy squished a raisin between her fingertips and nodded. "And I asked him to wait for one more day to reveal the truth. I am sorry, I know how difficult every day has been for you. I know how concerned you are about Claybrook, and you will not rest until he is proved innocent. But, please, can I have one more day?"

"And if I said, I can't bear waiting anymore?"

"I will ask him to reveal the truth at once."

"I can wait a few more hours, Lucy. I can do that for the sake of our friendship. We have been in this together since the beginning. I am not going to abandon you now."

Lucy leapt up and threw her arms around her. "Oh, I am so glad I found you. You are absolutely wonderful."

"And you are completely dotty. Who in the world says they love fruit cake and then proceeds to pick out the fruit before eating it? I have raisins stuck all over my dress now."

Lucy sat back feeling refreshed. "I am ready to tackle this murder business again. Now, what did Lord Adair say? Ah yes, he gave me a hint. He said that the target was both the men."

"What? Which men?"

"Lord Beazley and Lord Willoughby."

"The murderer wanted to kill both of them?"

"Yes."

"That means Lord Willoughby is not the murderer."

Lucy clapped her hands excitedly. "That's true. And, after speaking to Lady Willoughby this morning, I realised something else. The butler wouldn't have done it either."

"Why not?"

"If he killed Lord Willoughby, then Lady Willoughby would have married Claybrook. Once married, she would have dispensed with the butler, since she knows Claybrook is too clever to be cuckolded. Hence, keeping Willoughby alive is in the butler's best interest."

"Mary could have done it," Elizabeth said thoughtfully. "Because if Lady Willoughby marries Claybrook and the butler is let go then she has most to benefit. She loves him."

"But she has no incentive to kill Beazley and Adair said that the murderer wants both the men dead."

"The cook could have pretended to be drunk, I suppose, and mislead us into thinking that she was fond of Beazley."

Elizabeth grabbed her head. "I am getting a headache."

"What we need is a cup of tea and a whole lot of luck," Lucy said, getting to her feet.

The rest of the evening, they poured over the facts again, trying to recall every bit of information. They paced the room, lay on the couch, sat upright and slouched, but no matter what position their head was in, nothing new came to light.

The last rays of the sun dipped below the horizon and plunged them into sudden darkness.

"We have been talking for hours," Elizabeth said, lighting a candle.

"And we are no closer to the truth."

"I think we should eat something and go to bed. Perhaps, in the morning, things will be clearer."

∞ ∞ ∞

Lucy trudged to her room, feeling despondent. She would have to spend the night lying in her bed, rooting through her memories for clues.

She grasped the doorknob and stepped inside, a moment later, a hand clamped on her mouth, and she was slammed against the wall.

"How dare you write to those girls, you interfering little doxy!"

Lucy's eyes widened in terror as the butler's other hand came up to pin her neck to the wall.

"I am going to kill you," he raged softly. His hand left her mouth and ripped the back of her bodice. "But not yet."

He gave her a sickly smile as his eyes took in her figure. His intentions were clear, and her terror escalated.

Suddenly the temperature dipped, the windowpanes began rattling, and the hair on her arms rose.

An eerie wail started up, and the butler frowned.

Lucy's heart leapt in hope. She knew this feeling. This odd terror and the chills . . . they usually meant that the ghost of Aunt Sedley, whose brother had died in the last place she worked at, had arrived. Over the course of the investigation, they had become friends, if a relationship between a human and a ghost could be called that.

And yet, when Aunt Sedley disappeared saying she was off to get married, Lucy had wondered if it had all been a delusion. Perhaps, in times of stress, her mind conjured up images.

A moment later, she was proved right when Aunt Sedley popped her head over the butler and exploding into a cloud of anger when she spotted the butler's hand wrapped around her neck.

"The candle, Girl!" the spirit of Aunt Sedley urged, as the puffs of smoke gathered back to form her polished figure one again. "Use the candle."

"Hurry, Miss Trotter," Lord Beazley's ghostly head floated in front of her blurry eyes. "Burn the damn man and run."

Spinoza suddenly appeared in between Aunt Sedley and Lord Beazely's head. He let out a loud squawk and attacked the butler's head.

Lucy didn't know if she was seeing things, but rather than waste time questioning her vision, she did as she was told. She stretched her hand out and began searching while Spinoza kept the butler distracted by enthusiastically pecking his forehead.

Soon her fingertips touched the smooth, tallow candle sitting on the dresser. In a trice, she set the butler's breeches on fire, and the moment he began screeching in pain; she ran.

In her harried state, she could only think of one place where she would be safe — the music room.

She didn't know why she thought of that room, perhaps because she had spent the entire morning there with Elizabeth and it was upmost in her mind.

Once there, she crawled under the piano and lay her head on the cold wooden floor. Her heart was thundering, and her breath came in sharp shallow gasps.

Was he looking for her? Would he guess where she was?

Her hand flew up to touch her sore neck. It hurt to swallow.

"He is back in his room, sitting in a basin of water," Aunt Sedley's head appeared in front of her.

She closed her eyes and tried to stifle her sobs of relief.

The ghostly apparitions stared at her. She ignored them, choosing to believe they were a figment of her imagination.

Or perhaps, she was truly mad.

After what felt like hours she quietened down, feeling suddenly exhausted.

"Find my killer," Beazley whispered in her drowsy ear.

"Didn't you see him?" Lucy asked sleepily.

"He shot me in the back, silly."

"You silly," she retorted, her eyes feeling heavy. It was becoming difficult to think.

"I have to go."

"Stay a while," she begged. "It's warm in the room, and your presence makes everything lovely and cold."

"You are an odd one. People are usually frightened of the ghostly chill."

"I told you," Aunt Sedley replied proudly. "Nothing terrifies her."

Not true, Lucy wanted to say but didn't have the strength as she drifted off to sleep.

Chapter Thirty-Five

Lucy

Lucy opened her eyes and found everything appeared luminous and white as if she had died and got stuck in a cloud.

It took her a few moments to remember that she was sleeping under a piano covered with a white sheet, hence the odd lighting. The pain in her throat brought back memories of the last night's events, and she closed her fists and dug her nails in her palm. She didn't want to remember any of it.

A loud whisper startled her. Someone was in the room. She stilled and tried to hear what was being said.

The scent of cigar smoke filled the air, the expensive kind.

"Kill him," Lord Aston snapped.

"We need to wait," the valet responded. "Let Adair leave."

"I am running out of time," Lord Aston growled. "I might be dead by this evening, and you may decide not to carry out the plan. It was hard enough to convince you to kill Beazley. Ever since you have had that little girl, you have gone soft in the head."

Lucy gasped, and the sound echoed in the room like an ominous bell.

In a trice, the valet whipped away the sheet and dragged Lucy out from underneath the piano.

"Not a word," Lord Aston threatened her.

Lucy gulped and nodded frantically. Her mind was working furiously despite her fear. Lord Aston had asked the valet to kill Beazley, and now they were after Lord Willoughby. But why?

Elizabeth walked in just then. "I was looking for you," she began when something in the faces surrounding her made her pause.

"This is a pity," Lord Aston said, pulling out a small, mother of pearl pistol that looked oddly feminine in his old, gnarled hands. "But, for the best. Join her," he gestured towards Lucy.

"She isn't involved. Let her go," Lucy rasped.

"She is a smart one," the valet said, taking Elizabeth's arm and forcing her to stand next to Lucy. "We can't take chances."

"What are you going to do?" Elizabeth asked, turning pale as the truth dawned on her.

"Kill you," Lord Aston replied.

"You will be caught," Lucy cried. "Lord Adair is just a few rooms away, and the Duke is arriving today."

"I will tell them that I came upon the two of you discussing how to murder my son. You attacked me once you realised that I had heard your confessions and in self-defence, I shot you both."

"Lord Adair will never believe you," Lucy argued.

"He will never believe I was plotting to kill my own son."

"What's this?" the door opened, and the butler strode in.

"The girls were plotting my son's murder," Lord Aston said irritably.

"But I heard you say that no one would believe that *you* were plotting to kill your own son," the butler responded shrewdly.

The valet sighed and dragged the butler to stand next to the girls.

"What are we going to do with him?" the valet asked, pulling out a cravat from his pocket and tying the butler's hand.

"Do with whom?" the door opened, and Lady Willoughby floated in. At the sight of the tied-up butler and the girls at gunpoint, she opened her mouth to scream, but the valet was once again efficient. He swiftly tied a handkerchief around her mouth and made her join the rest.

"I might as well kill them all," Lord Aston snapped. "Parasites, the lot of them. I loathe her anyway. I hope my son decides to join us, as well, and I can finish the job myself, Perris. I am tired of waiting for you to do it. I can then hand over the gun to Miss Trotter and pretend she killed them all because she is a crazed loon."

The valet dragged Lady Willoughby forward. "Do you want to begin with her?"

Lord Aston shrugged. "I suppose since I despise her the most." He raised the gun and aimed it at her forehead.

"Ack!" the valet slapped a hand on his neck. His eyes rolled back, his knees crumpled, and he landed on the carpet in a dead faint.

Lucy peered at the man and found a tiny arrow sticking out from the side of his neck.

Lord Aston baulked in confusion. The gun wavered in his hand.

Lucy spotted Lord Adair leaping over the window ledge. His muscles rippled under his morning robe as he landed soft-footed and powerful like a panther into the room.

The sun rose in the sky, the clouds scampered, and sunlight streamed in, bathing the musical instruments in soft golden light.

The butler shouted for help and Elizabeth screamed.

Lucy leapt upon Lord Aston and began wrestling him for the gun.

Lord Adair walked up to the butler, who smiled at him in relief.

Lord Adair smiled back and smashed a violin on his head. The butler went down with a twang. Next, he twisted the cheetah head and flipped it open to reveal the head of a gun. He pointed it at Lord Aston. "Give her the pistol, old man," he commanded.

Claybrook, the maids and the cook rushed in just then. "We heard screams. What is going on?"

Aston sprang to his feet, proving surprisingly strong for Lucy. In the ensuing tussle, the pistol faced Claybrook standing open-mouthed at the doorway.

Elizabeth leapt into the air and landed in front of Claybrook just as a shot rang out.

"Elizabeth!" Claybrook howled. "Are you hurt?"

She stared at her arm, blood bloomed on her muslin sleeve and began to spread. She swooned, and he caught her in his arms.

"Enough," Lord Adair snapped and grabbed Lord Aston's wrist, twisted it and extracted the pistol. "Now, Claybrook, tie the old man up. As for the valet, I gave him a good dose. He will sleep for two days. Lock him up in a servant's room until the Duke arrives."

Claybrook blinked. "What on earth is going on?"

Lord Willoughby staggered into the room, holding a bottle of brandy. "A noisy morning," he slurred.

Lord Aston turned apoplectic at the sight. "Nincompoop! Why couldn't you have come in earlier? I would have shot you and be done with it," Lord Aston turned towards the sleeping valet. "I told you to kill him," he said, kicking him. "Wake up, you fool! I told you to kill him and now look at him. Wobbling around in a drunken haze, drowning our family wealth and status in brandy, snuff and cards."

"What is going on?" Lord Willoughby asked again, looking bewildered. "Why is the valet on the floor? Why is the butler moaning?"

"Into the drawing-room," Lord Adair ordered. "I will explain everything."

Chapter Thirty-Six

Lucy

The drawing-room was once again filled with members of the household. The ghastly pink room seemed to gleam in excitement as Lord Adair and Claybrook strode in.

Claybrook headed straight for Elizabeth sitting at the back of the room on a hard-wooden chair. He took her arm and led her to the sofa, his set face ignoring her protests.

To everyone's relief, the bullet had simply grazed Elizabeth's arm. Lucy had been delighted to see Claybrook looking like the world had ended around his proud ears at the sight of Elizabeth lying pale and still on the bed. She couldn't wait to tease her about it.

Lucy leaned against the mantelpiece, a smile on her face. They belonged together, she thought sappily. If only she could do something to make them see it.

She straightened in surprise when Lord Adair approached her. He turned his back to the room, hiding his actions with his broad back and reached out and ran a finger down her nape.

She winced and closed her eyes.

"Who did this?"

"The butler."

"The clothes?"

"He had r-ripped the back. I had to change."

He nodded. "I thought as much."

"Did he? Are you well?"

She flushed red and looked away. "N-nothing worse than this bruise. I escaped."

"Here," he said, handing her a pot of salve, "apply this the moment you get a chance."

"Did you bash him on the head with the violin because you guessed what had happened?"

"I bashed him, as you so poetically put it, because I felt like it."

"Thank you for the salve."

He nodded and walked towards the head of the room.

"I told George to kill Beazley," Lord Aston spoke before Lord Adair could.

Lord Willoughby sprang to his feet. "And you wanted to kill me too? Your own son? I heard you admit as much earlier."

"Oh, sit down, you watery headed looby. I deny nothing. I wish I had drowned you the day you were born. You have been nothing but a shame."

Lord Adair held up his hand. "Please, squabble later, and let me explain the facts to those present before the Duke arrives. Now, the valet, George Perris, shot Lord Beazley," he said, his eyes focusing on Lucy. "I knew the moment I met Lord Aston the first time that he was behind it."

"How?" Lucy asked in surprise.

"When you told me what had happened, it made me questions a few things, Miss Trotter. Why would a guest decide to go deep into a forest on a cold, snowy morning? Someone must have lured him out, which meant that they knew who they were dealing with no matter whose clothes he was wearing."

Lucy frowned thoughtfully. "And the fact that the valet found him is suspicious too. He dragged the body over to Gopshall Manor and announced the murder."

Lord Adair nodded in approval. "Just like Lord Beazley, what reason could the valet have of going to the forest, and how did he just happen to come across the body? The woodland is large, and the body lying was deep within it."

"I have been a fool," Lord Claybrook said softly. "The only footsteps I found during my investigations were of Lord Beazley and the valet. I gave the murderer more credit than he deserved. I thought he had managed to erase his footsteps somehow, when in fact, he had done nothing of the sort. The truth was right in front of me, and I never saw it."

"Next," Lord Adair continued, "I wondered if the valet had been acting of his own free will or was someone else behind it all. And then I met Lord Aston. He was sitting in the drawing-room surrounded by three roaring fireplaces. The heat was unbearable, and he wore only his unmentionables. That's when it struck me. Why does a man who detests wearing clothes have a valet? Besides, he could have easily hired a footman to carry him around, and it would have been easier on the pocket."

Lord Aston sighed, "I never had a chance against you did I, Adair? I had asked Perris to keep an eye on Beazley and Willy. I knew they were gambling, and once I realised how far in debt Willy had fallen, I had to get rid of Beazley."

Lord Adair pulled out a piece of paper from his pocket. "When I was in London, I procured this information. George Perris had been a tailor in London. He caught a man trying to kidnap his wife and murdered him in a fit of rage. He was due to be hanged when Lord Aston heard about him and procured his freedom by bribing the officials."

Aston nodded. "He knew a bit about clothes since he had been a tailor in a fancy shop in Mayfair. He had that look about him too, that dignified upper-class servant air. I paid well for his freedom, bought the witnesses, and set him free."

"And then you blackmailed him into working for you," Lord Adair replied.

"I did. A word from me and he would have been back behind bars, and his family would have been left destitute. He had to do as I said, but I did treat him well. I paid him handsomely and sent his children to school."

Lord Adair spoke coldly, "You have been getting Perris to steal the debt notes or kill anyone Willoughby had lost a fair sum to for years."

Aston took out a cigar and lit it with shaking hands. "Yes, and then the physician told me I didn't have long to live. I realised no one would be around to clean up his mistakes after my death. It's only a matter of time before Willy gambles away everything, perhaps, even the title. My grandson, little Johnny, would have been left impoverished. I couldn't let that happen."

"You could have cut him off," Claybrook snapped.

"That woman is shrewd," he pointed at Lady Willoughby. "She would have found a way to get the money. Perhaps, declared me insane and made my will redundant, or who knows what new plan she would have concocted. She is desperate and clever. If she could fool Richard at one point, she can fool anyone. No, the only way I could ensure that Richard got the title and all my wealth was by killing him off."

Claybrook sprang to his feet. "I want none of it. It belongs to William and if he wants to squander it, then so be it. How can you treat your own child so terribly?"

Aston scowled. "He has been useless from the moment he was born. He whined, whinged and moaned, unlike you. You should have been the eldest, not this snivelling gambler."

Adair held up his hand, and Claybrook closed his mouth and sat down. "The duke is a good friend of yours," he remarked.

Aston nodded. "I won't hang, but poor Perris will."

And then he pulled out a gun from his pocket and shot himself in the head.

Chapter Thirty-Seven

Elizabeth

Elizabeth sat on the bench in the gazebo and stared at the cupid. Someone had fixed it, and now a rush of water cascaded down from the pot he was holding. Her eyes filled with tears. It was the last time that she would see Lucy and Claybrook. Early the next morning, she was leaving to begin her new post as a companion to an old lady.

The accusations, the lies and the murder had filled her life with so many knots, and now that they had all unravelled, she felt bereft rather than relieved.

She realised that she would rather face the chaos again just so she could spend a few more days with Claybrook. It was a sobering thought. It made her realise how deep and intense her love was for him.

The iron door of the gazebo squeaked, and she spoke without looking up, "I knew you would come. Today is our last day together."

"Is it?" a male voice asked.

She sprang to her feet. "My lord . . . I thought it was—"

Claybrook walked up to her. "Lucy, I know. She sent me here. She told me Lord Adair wanted to talk to me about something rather urgently."

"He is not here."

"I can see that."

Elizabeth swallowed and backed a few steps. "I think I will go look for her."

"Stay."

"I cannot."

He moved towards her, his steps slow and careful, as if he was a hunter approaching a skittish deer.

"Elizabeth," he said, reaching out and gripping her chin. He forced her to look up and show her face. "I understand."

She burst into tears, and his arms enveloped hers.

"Hush," he soothed, pulling out the pins and running his hands through her hair.

They stayed in the embrace for a while and then his fingers began dancing on her skin; light as a feather, no longer soothing but disturbing.

Her chest rose and fell, and her breathing became laboured. She became aware of his heat and their closeness, his hands running gently down her back, his rough stubble against her cheek.

She couldn't help it; she stood on her tippy toes and kissed his neck.

His sharp intake of breath made her jerk away. He grabbed her sleeve and pulled her back into his arms; the cloth tore, exposing her shoulder but neither cared.

He bent his head and kissed her.

"I love you," she breathed against his lips.

"Oh, my goodness," Lucy cried.

Elizabeth looked over Claybrook's shoulder and paled.

Lucy, Lord Adair, Lady and Lord Willoughby, the cook and the butler stood gaping at them.

"Is this what you wanted to show me?" Lady Willoughby snapped at Lucy.

Lucy shrugged innocently. "I thought I saw an intruder here. Instead, we find these two in a very shocking and intimate embrace. This is a scandal. Poor, Miss Verney will be ruined unless Claybrook marries her."

"I won't say a word," Lady Willoughby responded quickly. "And he does not need to marry someone like her."

"Do you mean she is a laced mutton?" Lucy asked, placing a hand on her heart in mock surprise. "How could you, Lizzy? I thought you were a good girl."

"She *is* a good girl," Claybrook finally spoke. "It is not her fault."

"You took advantage of her?" Lucy gasped.

"No," Claybrook cried.

"Claybrook is a man," Lady Willoughby snapped. "He is bound to sniff after servant girls. No need for marriage and such foolishness. No one here will say a word. We will pretend it never happened."

"I shall not keep silent," Lucy cried, outraged. "I cannot believe the girl I trusted, my friend, Miss Elizabeth Verney is a . . . is a harlot."

Elizabeth's face flamed. She couldn't understand why Lucy was saying such things.

Lucy crossed her arms and glared at Elizabeth. "You are a doxy. How could you forget about your family? What if they find out? You would stoop so low for money, tsk tsk. I am shocked by your behaviour. You have deceived me. You are a lady of easy virtue, harridan and a goosecap moll!"

"She is no such thing!" Claybrook roared. "She is a wonderful, honourable woman."

"Her honour, sir, is lost," Lucy shook her head sadly. "Unless you mean to restore it. Otherwise, I will tell everyone what I saw, and Miss Verney will be ruined for life. She will be shunned by society. She will have to live in a small hut in the middle of a forest and live on leaves and berries and an occasional squirrel. Mayhap, if she is quick, a juicy duck—"

"I don't need you to tell me what to do, Miss Trotter," Claybrook snapped. "I want to marry her. I love her. I knew the moment she was shot that I would rather face the gossip than lose her forever."

Lucy giggled. "I think you just needed a little push to get on with the asking. You were taking too long."

Elizabeth's eyes widened. So, this entire scene was created by

Lucy to get Claybrook to admit his feelings. She glared at her friend, "Doxy, am I?"

Lucy smiled. "It worked, didn't it."

Claybrook pulled Elizabeth back into his arms. "You can talk to Lucy later," he said and kissed her again.

"The scandal," Lady Willoughby wailed. "He can't marry her!"

Lord Adair shrugged. "The fact that Lord Aston was behind a lot of murders in the past few years will overshadow who Claybrook marries."

Elizabeth wrapped her arms around Claybrook and tuned the rest of the objections out. If Lord Adair had given this union his blessing, then their wedding was inevitable.

Claybrook smiled against her lips, picked her up and took her back to the house to have his wicked way with her.

She did her best to encourage him.

∞∞∞

Lucy

Lucy oscillated in the gazebo, unsure of where to go. The case was solved, and she didn't work for the Willoughbys anymore, so she had no place in Gopshall Manor.

"The carriage is ready," Lord Adair's valet said from the door.

Everyone had retired to the house except Lucy and Lord Adair. She lifted her hand, and Spinoza swooped down and landed on her arm.

"Lord Adair," she called.

He hesitated a moment before turning around to face her.

"Do you truly believe no one will care about Claybrook marrying Elizabeth?"

Lord Adair gestured for her to follow. "I do. Although I don't think a marriage between them will work. She is a governess, while he is an aristocrat. I do not mean she is less worthy, but I do think that the difference in upbringing will affect their happiness."

"I think they will be happy."

"I have seen exceptions, the Fairweather sisters, for instance, but everyone cannot be so fortunate. I believe marriages should be conducted between individuals of similar social standing otherwise insecurities creep in."

"But, my lord, women are not considered equal to men. We are inferior beings, and the education we receive is not the same."

"That's utter nonsense. I believe men and women are equal at birth, but its grooming and education that sets them apart and makes one more powerful than the other. And for a fruitful relationship, equality in mind and status is necessary. I have seen numerous men claim credit for things accomplished by their wives or daughters, and it's a shame."

She didn't want to argue with him, so she changed the subject. "My lord, I did learn who the murderer is."

"By sheer luck."

"I have been lucky twice. Perhaps, you should keep me close lest my luck rubs off on someone else."

"I have never seen a more persistent and stubborn creature."

"Please," she batted her lashes at him. "Will you teach me how to thwack a man and shoot him dead?"

They reached the carriage, and he turned to face her. "You remind me of a delicate dandelion puff or a starved baby rabbit." He searched her face, his eyes intent and knowing.

"A good dinner will sort that out."

"A curious specimen who managed to survive the orphanage with hardly any scars here," he said, tracing her forehead.

"I don't understand."

"Your disposition has remained pleasant even though your experiences have been traumatic. You seek joy and fun even in difficult times. Happiness is more important to you than anything else."

"Err."

"Any other girl in your position would have asked me to find them a husband. You are asking me to teach you how to shoot a man instead."

"I—"

He held up his hand. "You take a trip across England in the middle of a snowstorm putting your life at risk, all because you cannot stand being accused of a crime you didn't commit. You did not mind risking your life as long as your name remained clear of any wrongdoing. It was not the noose but the thought of losing your self-respect that terrified you. Your name is important to you, Miss Trotter, since that is all you have."

Her eyes widened as he spoke. He understood her better than she knew herself. An odd sort of fear crept up the back of her spine as she stood looking at him. She wasn't sure if she liked the fact that he could read her so easily.

His eyes softened. "You never ask for help. You leap in with both feet and try to do everything yourself no matter how dangerous the situation. An untrained person is bound to die young with a nature like yours."

Her eyes lit up. Was he saying what she thought he was saying?

What was he saying?

She frowned.

"You make me laugh, Miss Trotter. So, for my amusement and your safety, I will train you. Just enough, so you survive to a ripe old age."

"I-I cannot accept charity. Can I pay you somehow? Perhaps, be your cook or maid?"

"You can be my housekeeper. Once, you are trained and ready, I will set you loose in the world again."

She leapt into the carriage before he had finished speaking. "To Lockwood it is!" she cried, bouncing on the seat.

"Your luggage," he told her, "will follow in the other carriage."

She smiled at him. "Lord Adair, you are wonderful."

He flushed at the compliment.

"I wanted to ask you one last, itty bitty thing," she said. "I promise to stay silent thereafter like a good housekeeper."

"What is it?"

She touched the bruise on her neck, and her eyes became clouded. Her terror was still fresh in her mind, and she knew it would be a long time before she would sleep peacefully again. "I am worried about the butler. I will be safe from him, but what of others? You had promised to teach him a lesson if he harmed a woman again. And he tried to kill me. Will you punish him?"

He patted her hand. "I took care of that."

"How?"

He rested his head on the back of the soft leather seat and closed his eyes. And just when she thought he had fallen asleep, he said, "I poisoned his tea, Miss Trotter. He will be dead by to-morrow morning."

The end

About the Author

Anya Wylde lives in Ireland along with her husband, sons and a fat French poodle (now on a diet). She can cook a mean curry, and her idea of exercise is occasionally stretching her toes. She holds a degree in English literature and adores reading and writing.

To be the first to hear of any new releases by Anya Wylde email her at anyawylde@gmail.com

Copyright:

OTHER BOOKS BY THE AUTHOR
Regency Romantic comedy
Penelope
Seeking Philbert Woodbead
Dorothy
Regency Mystery
Wicked Wager
Murder At Rudhall Manor
Fantasy Novella
Ever After
Contemporary Romantic Comedy
Love Muffin And Chai Latte
Goodness Gracious Gracie